Virtual

Vampires

of

Vermont

Here's what readers from around the country are saying about Johnathan Rand's *AMERICAN CHILLERS:*

"Our whole class read POISONOUS PYTHONS PARALYZE PENNSYLVANIA, and it was GREAT!"

-Trent J., age 11, Pennsylvania

"I finished reading DANGEROUS DOLLS OF DELAWARE in just three days! It creeped me out!"

-Brittany K., age 9, Ohio

"My teacher read GHOST IN THE GRAVEYARD to us. I loved it! I can't wait to read GHOST IN THE GRAND!"

-Nicholas H., age 8, Arizona

"My brother got in trouble for reading your book after he was supposed to go to bed. He says it's your fault, because your books are so good. But he's not mad at you or anything."

-Ariel C., age 10, South Carolina

"Thank you for coming to our school. I thought you would be scary, but you were really funny."

-Tyler D., age 10, Michigan

"AMERICAN CHILLERS is my favorite series! Can you write them faster so I don't have to wait for the next one? Thank you."

-Alex W., age 8, Washington, D.C.

"I can't stop reading AMERICAN CHILLERS! I've read every one twice, and I'm going to read them again!"

-Emily T., age 12, Wisconsin

"Our whole class listened to CREEPY CAMPFIRE
CHILLERS with the lights out. It was really spooky!"
-Erin J., age 12, Georgia

"When you write a book about Oklahoma, write it about my
city. I've lived here all my life, and it's a freaky place."
-Justin P., age 11, Oklahoma

"When you came to our school, you said that all of your books
are true stories. I don't believe you, but I LOVE your books,
anyway!"
-Anthony H., age 11, Ohio

"I really liked NEW YORK NINJAS! I'm going to get all of
your books!"
-Chandler L., age 10, New York

"Every night I read your books in bed with a flashlight. You
write really creepy stories!"
-Skylar P., age 8, Michigan

"My teacher let me borrow INVISIBLE IGUANAS OF
ILLINOIS, and I just finished it! It was really, really great!"
-Greg R., age 11, Virginia

"I went to your website and saw your dogs. They are really
cute. Why don't you write a book about them?"
-Laura L., age 10, Arkansas

"DANGEROUS DOLLS OF DELAWARE was so scary that I
couldn't read it at night. Then I had a bad dream. That book
was super-freaky!"
-Sean F., age 9, Delaware

"I have every single book in the CHILLERS series, and I love them!"

-*Mike W., age 11, Michigan*

"Your books rock!"

-*Darrell D ., age 10, Minnesota*

"My friend let me borrow one of your books, and now I can't stop! So far, my favorite is WISCONSIN WEREWOLVES. That was a great book!"

-*Riley S., age 12, Oregon*

"I read your books every single day. They're COOL!"

-*Katie M., age 12, Michigan*

"I just found out that the #14 book is called CREEPY CONDORS OF CALIFORNIA. That's where I live! I can't wait for this book!"

-*Emilio H., age 10, California*

"I have every single book that you've written, and I can't decide which one I love the most! Keep writing!"

-*Jenna S., age 9, Kentucky*

"I love to read your books! My brother does, too!"

-*Joey B., age 12, Missouri*

"I got IRON INSECTS INVADE INDIANA for my birthday, and it's AWESOME!"

-*Colin T., age 10, Indiana*

AMERICA'S #1 SERIES FOR MAXIMUM CHILLS!

#13: Virtual Vampires of Vermont

Johnathan Rand

An AudioCraft Publishing, Inc. book

This book is a work of fiction. Names, places, characters and incidents are used fictitiously, or are products of the author's very active imagination.

Book storage and warehouses provided by Chillermania!©
Indian River, Michigan

Warehouse security provided by:
Lily Munster and Scooby-Boo

American Chillers #13: Virtual Vampires of Vermont
ISBN 13-digit: 978-1-893699-58-8

Librarians/Media Specialists:
PCIP/MARC records available **free of charge** at
www.americanchillers.com

Cover illustration by Dwayne Harris
Cover layout and design by Sue Harring

Printed in USA

Virtual
Vampires
of
Vermont

VISIT CHILLERMANIA!

WORLD HEADQUARTERS FOR BOOKS BY JOHNATHAN RAND!

Yooperland

Indian River

Alpena

Traverse City

MICHIGAN

CHILLERMANIA!

**I-75 Exit 313
then south
1 mile!**

Mt. Pleasant

Bay City

Grand Rapids

Lansing

Kalamazoo

Detroit

Visit the HOME for books by Johnathan Rand! Featuring books, hats, shirts, bookmarks and other cool stuff not available anywhere else in the world! Plus, watch the American Chillers website for news of special events and signings at *CHILLERMANIA!* with author Johnathan Rand! Located in northern lower Michigan, on I-75! Take exit 313 . . . then south 1 mile! For more info, call (231) 238-0338. And be afraid! Be veeeery afraaaaaaiiiid . . . .

When most people think of vampires, they think of someone like Count Dracula. You know . . . someone dressed all in black with pasty-white skin, with two fangs protruding over cherry-red lips. A creature that sleeps during the day and prowls the night, searching for victims.

And most people—myself included—know that vampires are only real in books and movies. Vampires just don't exist anywhere else.

But what if I told you that they really *do* exist? What if I told you that, yes, there really are vampires, that exist in another world . . . a world that is closer than you might think?

Would you believe me?

Because that's what this is about. Not just vampires . . . but *virtual* vampires. Vampires that are alive like you and me, living and breathing, walking and talking.

Now, I know what you're thinking. You're thinking that it's impossible. Hey . . . that's what I thought—at first.

But now I know the truth. And soon, you will, too.

My name is Mike Sherman, and I live in Stowe. It's a village in the state of Vermont. Lots of people vacation here, because there's all kinds of things to do . . . especially in the winter. Mt. Mansfield, which has the highest peak in Vermont, is a great place to ski and snowboard. In the winter, my friends and I go there a lot.

Something else I really like to do is tinker with computers. Oh, I use the computer for my homework and to play games, but I really like fixing computers and finding out how they work. When I grow up, I want to get a job repairing computers, or maybe even building them.

And that's how this whole thing got started: with a computer and a game.

I know it doesn't sound scary at all. But when you understand just what happened and why, you'll realize why I was so frightened.

The computer that I have wasn't working right. It was an older one that my dad gave me. He had bought a new computer, and said that I could have his old one. It seemed to work okay for a while, but then it started acting up. It would shut down all by itself, and sometimes it would freeze up and I would lose all of my homework that I had been working on. There was something wrong with it, but I didn't know what it was.

Which wasn't that big of a deal. I could fix it, I was sure. I didn't think it would be much of a problem.

And if I hadn't received a birthday gift in the mail, things probably would have turned out a lot different than they did.

I got home from school one snowy November day to find a small package waiting for me. It was a birthday gift, sent by my aunt and uncle in South Carolina.

Even before I opened it, I was sure of what it was. They had asked me what I wanted for my birthday, and I told them I wanted a new car, or a computer game. Well, of course they weren't going to get me a new car! It's a great trick, and it works.

I opened up the package, and sure enough . . . it was a game for my computer. It was called *'Return of the Vampire'.* On the front of the box was a picture of an old stone castle. It looked really cool, and I couldn't wait to play it. *Return of the Vampire* looked like it would be an awesome game.

But it wasn't.

It wasn't awesome . . . because it wasn't a game.

It was real—and my rollercoaster ride of terror was about to begin.

2

I took the game into my bedroom and turned on my computer. The screen flashed to life, blinked a few times, and then started up. The computer game was on a CD-ROM, and I placed it in the tray and slid it shut. I could hear it whir as it spun round and round.

Suddenly, the computer screen went black, and it stayed that way.

Oh, come on, I thought. *Not again.*

I tried tapping the keys, but nothing happened. I clicked the mouse, but that didn't work either.

Just then, Jenny, my little sister, came into my room carrying a Barbie doll. She's seven, and four years younger than me. Sometimes she can be a real pest, but usually, she keeps to herself.

"Whatcha doin'?" she asked.

"Trying to get this thing working," I replied.

"Did you break it?"

I shook my head. "No. It's just getting old, and it doesn't work like it used to."

Jenny saw the computer game box on my desk. "Eeewww," she said. "That looks scary."

"I hope it is," I said, still tapping the keys. The computer screen remained dark. "If I can ever get this thing working right."

"My Barbie doll works right," she said, holding her doll up for me to see.

"Yeah, but I don't play with dolls," I said, growing increasingly frustrated with the broken computer.

"It doesn't look like you're going to play on the computer, either," Jenny said.

"Look," I said angrily. "Don't you have something else to do?"

Jenny shook her head, and her hair slapped her cheeks. "Nope."

"Well, find something, or else I'm going to flush your Barbie doll down the toilet."

Jenny's eyes widened. The thought of her doll swirling down the toilet was horrifying. She spun and stormed off.

Well, that's one problem taken care of, I thought. *Now if I can only get this computer working.*

I turned the computer off, waited for a few minutes, then re-started it. While I was waiting, Mom came to my bedroom door. Jenny was standing next to her.

"Did you tell your sister that you were going to flush Barbie down the toilet?" Mom asked.

"I was only kidding," I said. "She was bugging me."

"Well, you apologize right now." Mom folded her arms, and if there's one thing I've learned in my eleven years, it's this: when Mom folds her arms, she means *business*. There's no point arguing with her when she's standing in front of you with her arms crossed.

"I'm sorry, Jenny," I said, even though I was mad at her.

"Tell Barbie you're sorry," Jenny said, holding out her doll.

Good grief, I thought, rolling my eyes. But if I apologized to her doll, maybe she would leave me alone. "I'm sorry, Barbie," I said, looking at the doll.

That seemed to satisfy both Mom and Jenny, and they walked away.

I worked on the computer for an hour, and I still couldn't get it to work. Soon, it was time to eat. The four of us—Mom, Dad, Jenny, and I—had dinner.

Jenny and I washed the dishes, and then I went back to work on the computer.

By bedtime, I still hadn't got it working right. I could get the machine to turn on, but it kept freezing up, and then all I would get was a black screen. I was really bummed, because I wanted to play *Return of the Vampire*. I guessed I would have to wait until tomorrow to get the computer working.

Sometime in the night, I was awakened by a noise. It was a whirring sound, like a gentle hum. As I emerged from my sleep, I realized what it was.

My computer. I recognized the sound instantly.

But that's impossible!

It had turned on . . . all by itself!

I was confused. How did the computer turn itself on? I mean . . . I knew that it wasn't working right, and it was freezing up. Sometimes, it would even turn itself off.

But who ever heard of a computer turning itself *on?*

From where my bed was, I couldn't see the monitor, but the glow from the screen reflected against my bedroom wall. I pulled down the covers, slipped out of bed, and walked to my desk.

On the screen was the same brick castle that was on the box of the computer game. The words *Return of the Vampire* were at the top of the screen, and, at the bottom, the words *Play* and *Exit.*

How did this thing turn itself on? I wondered. I had worked on the computer for hours and didn't have any luck, and now, in the middle of the night, the computer had turned itself on and loaded the game . . . all by itself.

For a moment, I just stared at the screen. The brick castle sat alone, cold and dark. I wondered about the game and how it was played. I had read books about vampires, but I had never played any games. I was sure that this game was going to be really cool.

But it was late. If I played the game right now, I would be really tired when I got up in the morning. Not to mention the fact that if Mom or Dad found me playing a computer game in the middle of the night, they would probably take the computer away from me.

By moving the mouse, I placed the arrow-shaped cursor over the word *Exit*. I clicked it twice, and the castle vanished. Then I shut down the computer and went back to bed.

But something still bothered me.

How did the computer turn on all by itself? I didn't think it was possible. I've heard of computers that turn off all by themselves, but they're programmed to do it. I've never heard of a computer programmed to turn on by itself.

And in the morning—you guessed it—the computer was on! Only now, there were two words written on the screen. White letters in front of a black background read:

I'M WAITING.

It was kind of eerie. Who was waiting? For who?

I moved the mouse and the letters vanished. The image of the castle appeared.

Return of the Vampire. Play. Exit.

I left the computer on and went into the kitchen. Dad was at the table reading a newspaper and sipping coffee. Mom was drinking tea and watching a small television set on the top of the fridge. Jenny was eating a bowl of cereal.

"That computer you gave me sure is acting weird," I said to Dad.

He looked up from his paper. "That's why I gave it to you," he said.

"No," I replied. "I mean, it comes on all by itself. It happened last night. I shut it off, but it did it again."

"Hey, it's better than nothing," Dad said without looking up from the newspaper.

"Maybe it's stuck on," Mom said.

I shook my head. "No. If that was the case, it would be impossible to turn it off."

I went back into my bedroom and shut off the computer. Today was another school day, and I didn't have time to fool around with the computer. I'd have to wait until I got home to work on it.

And as I rode the bus, that is what I figured I would do. After school was over, I would go home and find out just what was going on with the computer. I would fix it, and then I would finally be able to play the game.

Return of the Vampire.

Of course, if I knew then what I know now, I would have thrown that computer game—and the entire computer—into the lake.

And it all began when I got home and went into my bedroom. It was then that I realized something was really, really wrong.

Mom and Dad both work, and Jenny stays after school, which means that I get home first. Which is kind of cool, because that means that nobody is around to bug me if I'm busy working on something.

When I got home, I walked straight into my bedroom. Once again, my computer had turned itself on all by itself.

But that wasn't the weird part.

The weird part was what was on the screen. Big letters read:

MAY I COME IN?

That's all it said. The words remained in the center of the screen.

I sat down at my desk and moved the mouse. Instantly, the words disappeared. The castle came into view, along with the words *Play* and *Exit*.

Well, might as well play, I thought, hoping that the computer wouldn't crash.

I clicked *Play*. Nothing happened for a moment, and then the screen went dark.

Suddenly, white letters appeared on the black screen.

YOU DIDN'T ANSWER ME. MAY I COME IN?

What in the world? I thought. I placed my fingers on the keys and spoke as I typed. "No," I said.

What happened next was bizarre. The screen went black again, and there was a loud popping sound. Then there was an electrical buzz and a hum. The computer shut itself off.

Terrific, I thought. I had been hoping that the computer might somehow fix itself, but that wasn't going to happen.

I reached down and turned the computer on. I could hear it whir and begin to start up.

"Hey Mike!" a voice shouted from outside. "You home?!?!"

It was Hayley Winthrop. Hayley lives next door, and she's in the same grade I am.

I stood up and looked out the window. Hayley was standing in the yard, facing our house. Snow was falling.

"Yeah!" I yelled loudly so she could hear me through the closed window. "I'm trying to fix this dumb computer! Come on in!"

I sat back down and heard the front door open, and soft footsteps padding across the living room floor. Then my bedroom door opened, and Hayley came in.

"What's wrong with it?" she asked, standing next to my desk.

"I don't know," I replied, shaking my head. "It's acting weird. I got a new game called *Return of the Vampire,* and I really want to play it."

The computer was up and running again, but the screen was black.

Suddenly, words began to form.

WHO IS YOUR FRIEND?

I gasped.

"How . . . how did it know you're here?" I stammered. I scooted my chair back from the desk.

"What's that?" Hayley asked, pointing at the screen.

I shook my head. "I don't know. But it's acting like it knows that you're here."

"That's impossible," Hayley said. "It's just a computer."

NO, I'M NOT.

Hayley and I gasped.

"It . . . it heard me!" Hayley exclaimed.

Now I was getting scared. I've never heard of a computer that could actually respond like that.

I reached down and pressed the on/off button. Nothing happened.

I pressed it again. Still nothing.

"Well, there's another way to shut it off," I said. I knelt down and reached behind the desk . . . but what I found sent waves of chills through my body.

"No!" I exclaimed. *"It's impossible! It's just not possible!"*

"What?" Hayley asked. "What's wrong, Mike?"

I held up the power cord, displaying the three prongs.

"It's not plugged in," I whispered. *"The computer is on . . . but it's not even plugged into the wall!"*

I double-checked, just to make sure that I hadn't grabbed the wrong cord.

Nope. The cord I had in my hand was connected to the back of the computer . . . and the computer was still on.

"Is . . . is there a battery in that thing?" Hayley asked.

I shook my head. "No," I answered. "There aren't any batteries in it."

"Then why is it still on?" Hayley said. Her voice quivered a tiny bit, and I could tell that she was more than a little nervous. I was, too.

"I don't know," I said.

The screen suddenly blinked to life. The castle appeared, along with the words *Play* and *Exit*.

"This is really strange," I said.

I sat down in my chair.

"What are you going to do?" Hayley asked.

"I'm going to play," I said. "I'm going to play the game and see what happens."

I moved the mouse and held the cursor over the word *Play*. Then I clicked.

The image of the castle faded slowly. Words appeared on the screen.

PLEASE ENTER YOUR NAME.

I entered my name by typing the keys.

PLEASE ENTER YOUR FRIEND'S NAME.

I typed in Hayley's name.

WELCOME, MIKE AND HAYLEY. ARE YOU READY TO PLAY?

I typed in the word *'yes'*.

PLEASE WAIT A MOMENT.

We waited. Nothing appeared to be happening.

Suddenly, a face on the screen began to appear. It was faint at first, but as we watched, it became clearer.

It was the face of a vampire . . . sort of.

It was a boy, maybe about my age. His dark hair was slicked back, and his face was very white. His eyes were two orbs of black coal. Two sharp fangs were barely visible at the corners of his mouth.

And he spoke.

"Welcome, Mike and Hayley. Are you ready to play my game?"

I was about to type in the word 'yes', but the face on the screen spoke again.

"There is no need to type your response," the vampire said. *"All you need to do is speak."*

I raised my eyebrows. "Okay," I said. I couldn't help but have the strange feeling that the face on the screen could actually see us. Plus, I was still freaked out that the computer was running without electricity.

"Good," the face said. *"Now . . . place your hands on the screen."*

I raised my hand and was about to place it on the screen, but Hayley grabbed my arm and stopped me.

"Wait," she said. "I'm scared. I don't like this."

I looked down at the unplugged cord on the floor.

"Well?" the vampire said.

Hayley shook her head. *"I don't want to play,"* she whispered. *"I think we should shut the thing off."*

"It's too late," the vampire said with a laugh. *"Oh, it's much too late for that."*

Without warning, two hands lunged out from the computer screen! One hand grabbed my arm, and the other hand grabbed Hayley's arm. Then we were being pulled!

Hayley screamed, and I started yelling. *"Let me go!"* I shouted. *"Let go!"*

But it was useless. The hands were too strong. I know it sounds impossible, but we were being pulled into the computer!

It was then that I realized that we were no longer playing a game. *Return of the Vampire* wasn't a game—it was reality.

And our reality had just changed.

We were about to discover that we were no longer in the real world, but a different world altogether. A virtual world, where things existed that were beyond our imagination.

A horrifying world . . . of virtual vampires.

Being pulled through the computer monitor was a really weird experience. I say 'weird' because it didn't really hurt at all . . . I just had this squeezed feeling, like I was being pulled through a tight tube.

And it didn't last long, either. In less than two seconds, I was no longer standing in my bedroom. Hayley appeared next to me like magic, and we looked around.

We were standing in a field. The sky was overcast and gray, the color of cold iron. A strange fog hung in the air. Behind us was a dark forest, and in front of us was a long, low sloping hill. At the top of the hill—

"Mike!" Hayley gasped. "That's . . . that's—"

"—that's the castle we saw on the computer screen!" I finished. "The one from the game!"

"How did . . . how did this happen?" Hayley stammered.

I could only shake my head. After a moment, I brought my hands to my face and rubbed my eyes. I was sure I was dreaming.

But when I opened my eyes, nothing had changed. The forest was still behind me, and the castle still loomed above us on the hill.

Suddenly, I heard a noise . . . like the soft padding of feet through grass. I turned, and so did Hayley.

We both jumped.

The vampire! The one that we'd seen on the screen—the one that had somehow pulled us into the computer—was coming toward us! He'd been standing near an old tree, and we hadn't seen him at first. He looked like he was probably about my age, only his skin was a lot whiter. And his hair came to a 'V' on his forehead. A dark cape draped over his shoulders, and he wore dark slacks and dark boots.

And he was *laughing!*

"You should have seen your faces!" he chortled, flashing a grin that showed a row of white teeth—and two sharp fangs.

"We've got to get away!" Hayley exclaimed.

"Please," the vampire said as he came closer. He slowed, and he raised his hands calmly. "Let me explain. I didn't mean to scare you. Let me just explain myself."

Fat chance of that!

"Run!" I shouted, grabbing Hayley by the wrist. *"Come on!"*

We broke into a sprint, heading for the dark forest. I figured that we might find someplace to hide there.

"No!" the vampire shouted from behind us. *"Don't run! I won't hurt you! I promise!"*

We weren't going to take any chances. After all, he was the same vampire that had pulled us into this weird world in the first place. There was no telling what he might do.

One thing I was glad about: we were a lot faster than the vampire. When I looked back over my shoulder, I could see that we were leaving him behind.

"Into the woods!" I huffed. "We can find someplace to hide in the woods!"

We darted around trees and branches. The forest, with its tall trees and thick limbs full of leaves, was even darker than I thought. It didn't take long to find a place near a stump where we could duck down in the shadows and hide.

"Right there!" I said, and Hayley and I rolled to the ground and snuggled up next to the old trunk, hoping to be hidden by the shadows.

We didn't speak. The only thing we did was huff and puff, trying to catch our breaths. I was sure that, at any moment, I would hear the crunching footsteps of the vampire coming toward us.

But I didn't.

"We're . . . safe," Hayley whispered, gasping under her breath. "We . . . got . . . away."

Hayley was right. We had escaped from the vampire.

But in the dark forest, there was something *else* that we had to worry about . . . and we were about to find out exactly what it was.

7

A hissing, squeaking sound.

We both heard it at the same time, but we couldn't tell where it was coming from.

"What was that?" I asked. Hayley didn't reply.

Suddenly, we heard it again. A shrill, high-pitched squeak that came from above. Then a dark shadow suddenly swooped down at us!

We were both still kneeling on the ground. I rolled to the side. Hayley shrieked and ducked down, covering her head with her hands.

Another dark shadow dove at us, and again, we had to move quickly to get out of its way.

Then, silhouetted by the evening sky, I saw what they were:

Bats!

There were at least a dozen of them, swarming above us, arcing up and down like mad hornets.

"They're bats!" I shouted. *"Stay down!"*

We hunkered as close as we could to the old stump. Bats were swooping and diving, and I was sure that at any moment, one of them was going to get caught in my hair . . . or worse. I'd heard that bats don't really hurt humans, but I wasn't taking any chances.

Besides . . . we had just been pulled through a computer screen! Who knew what might be possible?!?!

I was scrunched down on the ground next to Hayley, wondering what to do, when I noticed that the bats weren't diving as much. I managed a quick glance up.

I could still see some dark shadows darting here and there, but the bats seemed to be leaving. Or, at least, leaving us alone. Their squeaks and squeals weren't as loud. After a few moments, the sounds of flapping wings and angry squealing were gone.

But then we heard something else.

Footsteps in the forest.

"I know you're here," a voice called out, and I knew that it was the vampire that we'd seen in the field.

"I didn't bring you here to hurt you," he continued. "Honest. I need your help."

"*You* brought us here, wherever we are," I said with distrust. "I don't know what's going on, but this doesn't seem like a game to me."

"I'm sorry," he said. "It's just that . . . well, I tried to get you to invite me into your world. Then it would have been easier."

What would have been easier? I wondered.

"When it didn't work, I realized that I would have to pull you into Virtuality on my own. But please . . . you don't have to hide. I can explain everything, and I won't hurt you."

He was really close now, and I wondered if he could see us.

And I wondered what to do. Was he telling us the truth? Or was he just saying that so we would come out of hiding?

"I know where you are," he said, and he was only a few feet away, I was sure, but there were so many trees that I couldn't see him.

"I won't come any closer," he said. "I just need you to listen to me. I need your help. If you listen and decide not to help, I'll show you the way back to your world. All I'm asking is that you listen."

Darkness seemed to close in. The thought of being lost in a strange forest—wherever we were—was almost as scary as the vampire.

"Okay," I said. "We'll listen. But then we have to go home. You have to show us the way back."

But when the vampire spoke and explained what was going on, I began to realize that getting back home was going to be difficult . . . if not impossible.

"My name is Ivan," the vampire began. "The castle is my home. You are now in the land of Virtuality."

"Virtuality?" I said. Next to me, Hayley shifted on her knees. I stood up, and Hayley did the same. From where we were, we could make out the silhouette of the vampire, clouded by the other shadows of the forest.

"Virtuality is a world created by a machine," Ivan continued. "It is my world. Or, it has been until a few days ago. Until they started arriving."

"Who's . . . who's *they?*" asked Hayley.

"Mutated vampires," Ivan replied.

"But . . . isn't that what you are?" I asked.

"Yes . . . and no. I am a vampire. But, as I said before, I will not hurt you. I was created, like

39

everything else in Virtuality, to be part of a larger universe. A world that blends your world with mine."

"You mean my computer game?" I asked.

"Sort of," Ivan said. "See . . . I am a vampire, but I won't hurt you. These vampires that have suddenly appeared . . . *they* are dangerous—to both you and me."

"But what about these other vampires?" Hayley asked. "Where did they come from?"

"I believe that there is a malfunction in the creation machine," Ivan replied from the shadows. "It's causing the vampires to mutate."

"You mean, like 'change'?" Hayley asked.

"Exactly," Ivan replied. "They look like vampires, but they seem to be half monster."

"This machine," I said. "You're talking about my computer, right?"

"Yes," Ivan said. "The creation machine—the computer. There is something wrong with it, and it is creating these awful vampires."

"A computer virus!" I exclaimed. "I'll bet that's what the problem is! My computer has been acting funny!"

"That's why I need your help," Ivan said. "As a virtual being, I don't know much about this computer that you speak of. But I do know one thing: more and more of these mutated vampires are being created every day."

"What's so bad about them?" Hayley asked. "I mean . . . besides the fact that they're vampires?"

"They're bad because—" Ivan started to say, but he didn't have time to finish his sentence. Suddenly, there was a crashing in the woods, like something running.

Something *big*.

In the next instant, a huge shadow appeared in front of us . . . and Hayley and I both knew that our worst fears were about to come true.

I was just about ready to run. Just *where* I would run, I hadn't a clue.

But I wasn't going to stick around to be attacked by a vampire!

"Zeena!" Ivan shouted into the dark forest. "I've been looking all over for you!"

The crashing sounds came closer. A dark shape suddenly leapt out from the shadows. I heard a whimper and a bark, and I knew right away that Zeena must be Ivan's dog.

What a relief! I thought we were about to be attacked by a mutated vampire!

"This is Zeena," Ivan said, as the dog sniffed Hayley and me. "She won't hurt you."

The dog plodded to where we stood. Even in the dark of the forest, I could see that Zeena was a Doberman. She was big, too, and she wore a leather collar with silver studs in it. I reached down to pet the animal, and she licked my hand. Then the dog walked over to Ivan.

"It will be dark soon," Ivan said. "We really shouldn't be in the forest with night approaching."

"Yeah," Hayley said. "Especially with all those bats that came after us."

"Oh, the bats here in the forest won't hurt you," Ivan said. "They're just ordinary bats. But—"

He didn't finish his sentence.

"But what?" I asked.

"I'll tell you later. Come on. Let's go back to the field where it isn't so dark. I'll explain more while we walk."

I realized that we really didn't have a say in the matter. We really had no idea where we were or what was happening. Here we were in a strange forest, in a strange world, and we didn't know why . . . yet.

But Ivan didn't seem like he wanted to harm us, which was a relief. He really did sound like he needed our help.

We started walking, following behind Ivan. Zeena ran up ahead of us. Branches and leaves crunched beneath our feet.

"Virtuality can only survive if there is enough energy and electricity," Ivan said as we walked. "The same goes for me, and everything else here."

"When you pulled us through the computer," I said, "it was on, but it wasn't plugged in. How can that be?"

"I don't know," Ivan said, shaking his head. "But there must be some energy source somewhere. That's what the mutated vampires want. Energy."

"Don't vampires drink *blood?*" Hayley asked.

Ivan laughed. "That's just an old fairy tale," he said with a chuckle. "I think someone wrote that to make vampires seem really scary. The truth is, virtual vampires need the same thing that all creatures of Virtuality need: energy. The problem is, the mutated vampires are using up all of the energy. If more of them come, they might take all of the energy in Virtuality. Then, my world will no longer exist. Virtuality will be no more."

"What would the mutated vampires want with us?" I asked.

"You are pure energy," Ivan replied. "Stronger than any other energy source in Virtuality. The mutated vampires will be even *more* attracted to you, because they'll want your energy. However, I knew that only someone from your world might be able to stop the mutated vampires. That's why I brought you into my world. But if the mutated vampires succeed in claiming your energy, then . . . ."

Ivan stopped speaking as we reached the edge of the forest. In the distance, I could see the silhouette of the huge castle on the top of the hill, curtained against the dark gray sky.

"What will happen then?" Hayley asked.

Ivan's answer chilled me to the bone.

"Then," he replied, turning toward us, "the invading mutated vampires will be unstoppable. Not only that, but they will have enough energy and power to leave Virtuality . . . and escape into your world. Then, nothing will stop them. You, and everyone in your world, will be in great danger."

That alone was scary enough.

"Well," Hayley began, "if you knew that the mutated vampires could do that, why did you risk bringing us here?"

"Yes, the danger is great," Ivan conceded. "But there is no other way."

However, when Ivan told us what we would have to do to stop the mutated vampires, I have never, ever been so scared in my life.

Now, you have to remember something:

Hayley and I are two ordinary kids, probably just like you. I couldn't believe what was happening . . . but, then again, I couldn't *not* believe it. Ivan's story sounded so crazy, so *bizarre* . . . but I knew well enough that what was happening was somehow *real*.

Somehow.

My gut feeling told me that Ivan was right. Somehow, we really *were* in Virtuality, a world created within my computer. We might even be a part of the game itself. I mean . . . in a weird way, it kind of made sense.

But there was something else I couldn't figure out.

My computer had turned itself on—and off—by itself. And I came home from school to find the computer on . . . even though it was unplugged. Computers can't work without electricity, period.

Weird.

"How are we going to stop the vampires?" I asked.

"Two things," he said. "It'll be night soon. We need to go to a market in Transylvania and get some garlic before nightfall."

"Transylvania?!?!" Hayley exclaimed.

"Oh, don't worry," Ivan replied. "It's not very far at all."

"What do we need the garlic for?" I asked.

"We need to bring garlic bulbs back to the castle," Ivan continued. "The mutated vampires are sleeping now, but when the castle bell rings and signals the arrival of nightfall, the vampires will awaken. We must find their coffins before it's too late. Then, all we have to do is open the coffin lid of each vampire and drop in a garlic bulb. The garlic acts as an energy magnet."

"You mean, like, it will drain the power from the vampire?" I asked.

"Exactly," Ivan said with a nod. "Once the vampire's energy is gone, the creature will shrivel up and vanish. That is why I need your help. I can't get close to the garlic, or the same thing will happen to me. I need your help collecting the garlic. And if we can get the garlic into the coffins before the mutated vampires awaken, we will succeed. There is, however, one thing that has happened that I must tell you."

Hayley and I were silent, and Ivan continued.

"It took a lot of energy to bring you into Virtuality . . . much more energy than I thought. So much energy that there might not be enough power for you to go back to your world. If we don't succeed in stopping the mutated vampires soon, all of the energy will be gone. Virtuality will no longer exist . . . and neither will you."

Oh no!

11

We had no other choice. We would have to help Ivan and stop the mutated vampires, before they became too powerful. I wasn't exactly sure what would happen if they escaped Virtuality and entered the *real* world, but I sure didn't want to find out. Neither did Hayley.

We were still standing at the edge of the forest. The sky was now a deep gray, signaling the coming night.

"Let's get started," I said. "How much time do we have?"

"About an hour," Ivan replied. "In an hour, the castle bell will ring, signaling the official arrival of night. Come on."

We walked along the edge of the forest until we came to a gravel road. Zeena was nowhere to be found.

"She runs off a lot on her own," Ivan explained. "But she always comes back."

"How far is Transylvania?" Hayley asked as we walked along the road.

"Not far," Ivan replied. "It's on the other side of a valley up ahead."

The farther we walked, the steeper the hills grew around the road. It was like the road had been cut out through a mountain, like we were walking in an empty river bed. I could make out dark shadows that looked like they might be caves. Actually, it looked a lot like where we live. Vermont has a lot of steep valleys and mountains.

But no vampires.

I looked up. The sky was a deep, slate gray, and I knew that it wouldn't be long before it was completely dark. I sure was glad that Ivan was with us. Being lost in Virtuality, all on our own, didn't seem like it would be a lot of fun.

"We're not very far now," Ivan said. "Actually, getting to Transylvania is pretty easy."

Seconds later, we found out how wrong Ivan was.

12

There was a sudden noise from behind us. At first, I thought that it might be Zeena. But when I turned and saw the enormous, dark shape, I knew that there was no way it could be a dog.

"What is *that?!?!*" I exclaimed.

"I . . . I don't know!" Ivan stammered. "I've never seen it before!"

At first I thought what was coming down the road was a giant snake. At least, that's what it looked like. But as it came closer, I realized that it was definitely *not* a snake.

It was a worm!

It was an earthworm . . . the biggest one I had ever seen. It was as big around as a truck . . . and it was slithering and slinking right toward us!

"Quick!" Ivan shouted. "Let's duck into a cave!" He darted to the side of the road to where the rock wall climbed up into the air. *"There are lots of caves around here!"* he exclaimed frantically. *"We need to find one that's big enough for us, but too small for that creature!"*

The three of us ran along the rock wall. Meanwhile, the giant worm was getting closer and closer. I was amazed at how fast it could move!

"Here!" Hayley exclaimed. "How about this one?"

Ivan turned. Hayley had found a cave that we could duck into. We'd have to stoop over to get inside, but it didn't look big enough for the worm to get through.

Hayley ducked down and slipped into the cave. I was next, followed by Ivan.

Inside the cave was totally dark. I mean *completely*. I couldn't see a single thing, except the mouth of the cave.

"You've never seen that thing before?" I asked.

"Never," Ivan said. "But a lot of weird things have been happening. I think it might have to do with the malfunction of the machine that created Virtuality."

Suddenly, the giant worm's head covered the entire mouth of the cave. Hayley screamed, and I cringed. The worm extinguished what little light there was. It was wriggling at the cave entrance, trying to get in.

"It knows we're here!" I gasped.

The three of us were frozen with fear. Normally, I would have never been afraid of an ordinary worm.

But, then again, I'd never seen a worm this big!

Suddenly, the worm backed away from the cave. It retreated back to the road, then stopped. It swung its head back and forth, around and around, like it was sniffing the air. I don't know if worms have noses, but that's what it looked like it was doing.

Finally, the worm stopped moving. Its long body stretched out along the road. It looked like it might have fallen asleep.

"Now what?" Hayley asked.

"Well, we can't go anywhere with that thing blocking our way," I said.

"But we can't stay here," Ivan said. "We've got to get to the village, get the garlic bulbs, and get back to the castle before nightfall."

We watched the worm for a few minutes, but it showed no sign of moving. Every few seconds it would raise its head, like it was looking around or something. But it didn't appear to have any eyes.

"We've got to go," Ivan insisted. "Time is being wasted. We've got to get to Transylvania."

"But that . . . that . . . *thing,*" Hayley stuttered. "How are we going to get past it?"

"I have an idea," Ivan said.

And when he told us what his plan was, I thought that he was crazy.

I also knew that it wouldn't work, and I began to realize that we weren't going to make it out of Virtuality, after all.

"Here's what I'll do," Ivan began. "I'll sneak out and go around the worm from behind. When I get to the other side of the road, I'll find another cave I can get into. Then I'll start making lots of noise to draw the attention of the worm. Hopefully, he'll come after me. I'll duck down into one of the smaller caves. Meanwhile, you two can sneak out of here and head to Transylvania."

"That's crazy!" Hayley exclaimed.

"Crazy or not, we've got to do something," Ivan said. "When you get to Transylvania, you'll see a small market just as you enter the village. Tell the owner that you need a big bag of garlic. Tell him that you need it to help me. He'll give it to you."

"But . . . but what about you?" I said.

"Never mind me," Ivan replied. "I'll be all right. Hopefully, by the time you get back the worm will be gone. Or maybe I can sneak away."

"Why don't the three of us try and sneak away right now?" Hayley asked.

"Too risky," Ivan said, shaking his head. "If something happens to all of us, then it's all over for Virtuality."

"Why can't we get some people from Transylvania to help?" I asked.

"Yeah!" Hayley exclaimed. "Let's get some other people to help us!"

"The people in Transylvania can't leave the village," Ivan said. "Remember: this world was created by a machine. Or, as you say, a 'computer'. The laws of Virtuality can't be broken."

I thought about that, and I realized that he was right. When you play a computer game, you have to play by the rules, otherwise, you lose.

And the more I thought about it, the more I thought that Ivan's plan just might work. The worm didn't seem like it was very fast, so if Ivan could distract it for a moment, that would give Hayley and me enough time to leave the cave and run down the road without the worm seeing us.

"Okay," I said. "Let's try it."

We crept toward the mouth of the cave. The sky above was growing darker and darker, and I knew that nightfall was quickly approaching.

"This will work," Ivan said confidently. "I'm going to follow the edge of the road way down past the tail of the worm, and sneak back up on the other side. Then I'll start making some noise. When the worm moves in my direction, you two take off down the road."

"Got it," I replied.

"Be careful," said Hayley.

Ivan tiptoed out of the cave and began walking along the edge of the rock wall. After a few moments, he vanished in the shadows.

"Man, I hope this plan works," I said quietly.

And the plan might have worked . . . but there was one thing that was about to happen that we hadn't counted on.

There wasn't anything we could do but wait, and as the seconds ticked past, I began to feel anxious. So far, the worm hadn't moved much, so I figured that Ivan was doing a good job sneaking around it.

Suddenly, his voice echoed from the rock walls.

"Hey! Worm! Over here! Over here!"

The worm's head jerked up and around, and immediately the gigantic creature began squirming in the direction of Ivan's voice!

"It's working!" Hayley said excitedly. "The worm is going after Ivan!"

Hayley and I stepped from the mouth of the cave, ready to sprint down the road. The worm was wriggling toward Ivan. We could see him now, a dark form on the other side of the road, jumping up and down and waving his arms. His cape rose up and billowed down behind him.

"Go!" Ivan shouted. *"Go now! He's coming after me! Now's your chance!"*

Hayley darted onto the road. "Come on, Mike!" she shouted. "Let's get going!"

I took a giant leap and bounded next to Hayley. Behind us, the giant worm was still wriggling toward Ivan. Ivan was still making lots of shouting noises, waving his arms to keep the attention of the enormous creature.

And for the first time, I could see the worm in its entirety. It reminded me of a train . . . only one without cars hooked together. I have never seen a worm look so terrifying and deadly.

"Let's go!" I said.

But as soon as we started to run, we heard Ivan's terrified screams, and we knew that, this time, he wasn't shouting to distract the worm. He was screaming in terror—and when I stopped and turned to see what was wrong, I gasped.

There was another worm coming out of the very cave that Ivan was going to hide in!

He was trapped!

We had to do something, but we didn't know *what*. Both worms were going after Ivan, and he had nowhere to run. In seconds, one—or both—of the worms might gobble him up.

"Make some noise!" I said to Hayley. "Maybe we can get the attention of one of the worms! It's our only chance!"

We started shouting and jumping up and down, but the worms didn't pay any attention. Both of them were focused on one thing:

Ivan.

The worms drew closer and closer to him. We could see Ivan desperately searching for an escape route, but there was none. He was trapped.

Suddenly, both worms lunged . . . *at each other!* They narrowly missed Ivan, who stepped aside just in time. The worms began fighting each other, rolling around, attacking one another, wrapping around each other like gigantic wires.

It was the break that Ivan needed. In a flash, he ran up to the rock wall. From there, he was able to bound away from the fighting worms and run toward us.

"Hurry!" I shouted. *"Before they see you!"*

Ivan ran as fast as he could. I could see his dark cape whipping behind him as he fled the horrific scene.

And the worms continued battling one another. It was really crazy to see! I felt like I was watching one of those old-time monster movies on television.

Ivan ran up to us, panting and out of breath.

"That was too close!" he exclaimed, huffing and puffing. "I thought I was history!"

"So did we," I said, still watching the raging worms.

"Let's get out of here before they come after us," Ivan said, and we took off running down the road, heading for Transylvania.

As we ran, I tried to imagine what the village looked like. I knew that there was an actual city called Transylvania in the country of Romania. But I had never been there, and I didn't know much about it, except that Dracula's castle was there.

But, then again, we weren't in the 'real' world. We were in Virtuality, a world that existed in my computer. I had no idea what we would find in Transylvania.

But I knew this much:

When we approached the village and I saw the look of terror on Ivan's face, I knew that something was horribly wrong.

The village was in shambles.

Houses had been knocked down, roofs had caved in. Even in the fading twilight, we could see that nearly every building had been severely damaged. There were pieces of houses—boards, shingles, entire walls—strewn all over the place. Several small buildings looked like they'd been hit by giant bowling balls. Carriages and wagons had been knocked over. Some of them were crushed. It was like a hurricane or a tornado had passed through.

We stopped and stared. There were no people around anywhere. Nothing moved. Transylvania looked like a ghost town.

"What happened here?" Ivan asked in bewilderment. Of course, Hayley and I didn't have an answer. If Ivan was confused, we were equally flabbergasted.

"Everything is wrecked," Hayley said, looking around. "It's like there was an earthquake or something."

"Has this ever happened before?" I asked Ivan.

He shook his head. "No. Never."

We stood staring for a few moments, and then Ivan started walking. "Come on. The market is right around the corner . . . if it's still standing."

We walked along a cobblestone street until we came to a building on the corner. It, too, was badly damaged. There was a sign above the door, but it was broken, and I couldn't read what it said.

And there were no lights in the village. With darkness approaching, it was difficult to see inside the market.

"Can we turn on any lights?" I asked.

"There is no electricity in the village," Ivan replied. "Only gas lights or candles, which I'm sure we can find in the market."

With Ivan leading, we entered into the dark market. We hadn't gone very far when we heard an old man's voice.

"Stop right there!" he said. His voice surprised us, and we did what we were told.

Suddenly, there was the sound of a match being struck. A tiny yellow flame appeared in front of us, and we saw an old man's face reflected in the glow. He touched the burning match head to a candle wick, and it flared to life. Then he shook the match out.

"What do you want?" the old man asked gruffly.

"What happened here? In the village?" Ivan asked.

The old man shook his head. *"What happened?!?!"* he replied remorsefully. *"What happened?!?! It was the work of those infernal worms!"* he said, as if we were supposed to know what he was talking about. "They came out of nowhere. Destroyed the town, they did. Everybody left. They were too afraid that the worms might come back. Say," he continued, looking at Ivan curiously, "you're that boy who lives in the castle, aren't you?"

"Yes," Ivan replied. "I'm Ivan. This is Hayley, and this is Mike."

Hayley and I nodded.

"We need your help," Ivan said. "Something is very wrong in Virtuality."

"You're not kidding," the old man said. "All of Transylvania has been destroyed by giant worms!"

"I don't know where they came from," Ivan said. "There's something really weird going on. More mutated vampires are appearing. We have no idea

71

where they are coming from, but they're draining too much energy from Virtuality. We're going to try and stop them."

"I've never seen anything like this before," the old man said sadly.

"Neither have I," Ivan said. "But we need your help. We need garlic."

"What?" the old man exclaimed. "Garlic? But you're a vampire!"

"I know," Ivan said. "That's why I brought my friends. I can't get close to the garlic, but Mike and Hayley can. Do you have any?"

"This way," the old man said, and we followed him through the dark market until we came to a long table. The table was filled with all sorts of fruits and vegetables.

"Here's the garlic you're looking for," the old man said, picking up a large garlic bulb. It was big . . . bigger than any other garlic bulb I had ever seen. Most of them are about the size of a golf ball. This one was the size of a softball!

Immediately, Ivan took a cautious step back.

"Oh, yeah," the old man said. "Sorry. You're a vampire. You can't get too close to this stuff."

"I'll be okay if they're in a bag," Ivan said. "A big bag. One that will hold a lot of garlic bulbs."

"Hold on a minute," the old man replied. "I think I've got a big leather bag in the back."

The old man walked away, leaving the three of us in darkness.

"If the garlic drains you of energy," Hayley began, "how come it doesn't drain energy from the old man? I mean . . . he's virtual, just like you, isn't he?"

"Yes, he is," Ivan replied. "But garlic only has that effect on vampires. No one else. That's why I'm sure we can stop the mutated vampires."

"Well, there's a good chance that the vampires are being created by a computer virus," I said.

"But what about the worms?" Hayley asked. "Are they caused by the same computer virus?"

I thought about it for a moment, and suddenly—

"Hayley! That's it!" I exclaimed. *"I know what those worms are!"*

17

As I began to realize that we actually *were* in a world that had been created by my computer, I began to establish some facts. Somehow, a virus in my computer was creating mutated vampires. But if a computer virus was to blame for the trouble—

"What?" Hayley replied.

"The worms!" I exclaimed. "They aren't *real* worms . . . they're *computer worms!*"

"You mean they are some sort of virus?" she asked.

"Exactly! They are computer worms that are messing up the system!"

"I'm not sure I'm getting all of this," Ivan said.

"A computer worm is really bad," I explained. "It's a type of computer virus, and there are many different

75

kinds. They can do really bad things to your computer."

"Which means they can do really bad things to Virtuality," Hayley said knowingly.

"Right!" I exclaimed. "Ivan . . . if I can somehow get into the internal workings of the computer, I might be able to stop not only the vampires, but the worms, too! Is there a way to get into the computer without actually leaving Virtuality entirely?"

"That's not a good idea," Ivan said, shaking his head. "No one from Virtuality has ever entered into the machine. If we entered into the machine, we would no longer exist."

"But you came through the screen," Hayley said.

"I didn't come *all the way* through," Ivan replied. "If I would have gone all the way through and entered into your world, I would have never been able to come back. My energy would be gone, and I would no longer exist. The mutated vampires, however, are different. They can survive anywhere there is pure energy. Me, I am limited by my own nature. I can never leave Virtuality."

"Yeah, but that's *you*," I said. "But the inside of the computer is part of *our* world! Part of the *real* world! Hayley and I wouldn't have any problem! Is there a way I can get inside to the inner workings of the computer?"

"There is a place in the dungeon of the castle," Ivan said. "There is a door into the machine where reality and Virtuality meet . . . so it *is* possible that you could enter into the machine without using much energy. But there's a problem."

"What?" Hayley asked.

"The bottom of the dungeon is covered with a terrible, acid-like slime. It seems to be coming from the door that leads into the machine. I touched it once, and it burned my fingers. "

I thought about that for a moment, trying to make some kind of sense of what I was hearing. Sure it was crazy, sure it was weird . . . but it was happening, and there had to be a reason for all of this madness.

"So, you think something might be leaking from the machine?" I asked.

Ivan nodded. "Yes, I think so."

"Let's go!" I said. "We don't need the garlic to stop the vampires if we can fix the computer problem from the inside!"

Ivan shook his head. "It will be too dangerous. If we get to the castle and the vampires are awake, they will sense your presence and come after us. They might stop us from ever reaching the dungeon. It will be best if we have the garlic . . . just in case."

The old man returned, carrying a lit candle in one hand and a large leather bag in the other. The leather bag was about the size of a grocery sack, and it was well-worn, with a leather drawstring used to close it. Hayley and I filled the bag full of large garlic bulbs while Ivan watched from a safe distance.

"Candles," Ivan said. "Do you have any candles?"

Again, the old man walked off into the darkness, only to return a moment later. He handed a candle to each of us, and then he gave Hayley a small box of matches. She shoved the box into her back pocket, along with her candle. We thanked the old man, and left.

As you can imagine, we were nervous as we left the village and began walking back to the castle. We had no idea if or when a worm might come after us, and now it was totally dark, so we couldn't see all that well.

We walked in silence until—

Ding, dong. Ding, dong.

Bells rang out in the distance. Their lonely chime echoed through the fields and forests.

It was officially nightfall. The mutated vampires would be waking up.

And we were headed straight to the place where they would be.

The castle.

I had thought I had been scared before. Being pulled into the computer was scary, and the bats in the forest had given us a fright. The strange, giant worms were even scarier.

But nothing we'd experienced so far could ever prepare me for what would happen to us inside the castle.

18

It was dark when we walked up the long, sloping hill and reached the castle. A billion stars peppered the dark canopy of night. There was no moon. In the forest, an owl hooted. Far away, coyotes bayed and howled, their shrieks fading quickly in the cool night air.

We stopped at a small bridge that went over a moat. A moat is a trench filled with water that circles a castle to keep people out. The only way to get to the castle is by a bridge that can be raised and lowered. When we arrived, the bridge had already been lowered.

"When night falls and the bell rings," Ivan explained, "the bridge is automatically lowered."

"By who?" I asked.

Ivan shook his head. "That's just the way it is. It's how the game is played."

I thought about that for a moment. *Return of the Vampire* was probably a really cool game—from the other side. If I was playing the game, and not *living* the game, it would probably be a lot of fun.

"Where is Zeena?" Hayley asked.

"Oh, she's free to roam around," Ivan replied. "She'll catch up with us soon."

Above us, the dark castle blocked out the sky. There were no lights anywhere.

"Okay," Ivan began. "There are a few things you need to know before we go inside. What you will experience will be the exact same things you experience when you play the computer game," he said.

"But we've never played the game," I said.

"Did you read the instruction manual?" he asked.

I shook my head. "I didn't get that far."

Ivan breathed a concerned sigh. "It's not going to be easy. You have to remember: this is real. When you play the game, it's just that: a game. But now you're in Virtuality, and everything is real . . . including the dangers."

"What other dangers?" Hayley asked, her voice heavy with worry.

"First of all, the mutated vampires," Ivan explained. "In the game, I'm supposed to be the only vampire in the castle. Now, however, there are mutated vampires inside. I don't know how many for sure. Maybe six, maybe ten. I just don't know."

That sounded bad enough, but Ivan continued. "There are also vampire bats in the castle."

"Vampire bats?!?!" I exclaimed.

"Nasty things," Ivan explained. "They will appear without warning, and we must be very careful."

"Yeah," Hayley said, "but they won't attack us, will they?"

"They will," Ivan said. "I can't explain everything to you now. But yes . . . they will attack us and try to steal our energy. However, since they are vampire bats, you can stop them with the garlic that you have in the bag. Garlic will drain the energy from the bats just like it will drain it from the mutated vampires."

"What else is in the castle?" I asked.

"Deranged cats," Ivan said, very matter-of-factly.

"What?!?!" Hayley and I exclaimed at the exact same time.

"If you were more familiar with the game, you would know this," Ivan said. "The deranged cats can become invisible, so you never know if one is around or not. They might seem small, but they can fight like tigers."

"Can we stop them with garlic?" Hayley asked.

"I'm afraid not," Ivan said. "Garlic doesn't have any effect on the cats at all. But the cat's aren't as vicious as the wolves."

I thought I was going to faint. "Wolves!" I cried. "There are *wolves* in there?!?!"

"Worse," Ivan replied. "Robotic wolves. They are mechanical, which is good . . . and bad. It's good because the wolves don't have the sense of smell or sight that 'real' wolves have. At night, they use tiny lights in their eyes to see. It's kind of like having built-in laser beams, but they can only see where the beam is being pointed. However, since the wolves are mechanical, they are also super-strong. They look just like real wolves . . . except their teeth are made of metal. I hope we don't run into any."

"You and me both," I said.

We were silent for a few moments, listening to the owl hooting and the cry of the coyotes far, far away. Finally, Ivan spoke.

"Ready?" he asked.

"I . . . I guess so," Hayley squeaked.

"Yeah," I replied, mustering as much inner strength that I could. "I'm ready."

Now . . . I *told* myself that I was ready. I spoke it out loud, and told Ivan and Hayley that I was ready.

I was wrong.

There was no way I could ever have been ready for what waited for us inside the vampire's castle.

19

The wood bridge creaked beneath our feet as we crossed over the moat. We approached the main door, which was very, very big. As we got closer to the castle, its immense size seemed to swallow us up. Looking skyward, the castle seemed to touch the stars.

Ivan pulled a candle from his pocket. "Do you have a match?" he asked Hayley.

Hayley dug into her back pocket and pulled out the small box of wooden matches that the owner of the market gave her. She struck the match against the side of the box and it flared to life. Ivan touched the candle wick to the flame and the candle glowed. Hayley shook the match out, then tossed it into the moat.

Ivan held the candle up. Before us, the castle door loomed. It was made of wood and iron. In the middle, there were two large, gray handles. Without a word, Ivan handed the candle to Hayley. Then he reached out, grasped the handles, and pulled.

Two doors parted in the middle and swung open with old, tired groans. Darkness awaited on the other side, empty and thick and heavy. Even the candle didn't provide enough light to see inside the castle. It was as if the doors led to a big cave, waiting to swallow us up.

"Maybe I'm not ready for this, after all," Hayley whimpered, handing the candle back to Ivan.

"We'll be all right," Ivan said. "But we'll have to be careful."

"I'll be glad when this is all over," I said.

"Me too," Ivan agreed, and he took a step into the castle. I followed, carrying the bag of garlic, and Hayley was right behind me.

"Where are we going to go?" I asked.

"I'll see if I can find the dungeon," Ivan replied.

"You mean . . . you don't know where it is?" Hayley asked.

"Sort of," Ivan replied. "You see . . . that's part of the way the game is played. Every time you enter the castle, the layout changes—meaning that rooms are never where they used to be, hallways and staircases are different."

"Don't you ever get lost?" I asked.

"I rarely leave the castle," Ivan replied. "The castle is designed to change so that it is more challenging for the person playing the game."

"So it's never the same when you go inside," I said.

Ivan nodded. "That's right. It makes the game more difficult . . . which means that it will be more difficult for us."

It was really weird to think that we were actually inside my computer, in another world that I never knew existed.

Ivan began walking, and Hayley and I followed close behind. I held the bag of garlic behind me as we walked, so it wouldn't be a danger to Ivan. The only sounds were the whispering of our shoes against the stone floor.

Soon, we came to another hallway, and Ivan stopped. Ahead of us the dark passageway continued on, and to the left of us was another corridor.

"Which way?" I asked.

"I don't know," Ivan replied, shaking his head. "Remember: everything is different. This hallway might be a dead end, or it might lead to a room. Or to another hallway. You guys light another candle and stay here, and I'll go this way to see where it goes."

"But what if you're attacked by a vampire?" I asked. "We have the garlic, and we won't be able to help you."

"The vampires will be drawn to you before they are drawn to me," Ivan answered. "You have a lot more energy than me. Just keep the garlic with you."

Somehow, I wasn't really comforted by that.

Hayley pulled her candle from her back pocket. Then she reached out and touched the wick to Ivan's candle, and it flared to life. Our faces glowed in the dim, yellow light.

Ivan turned and began walking down the corridor. All we could see was the tiny bead of the candle as it grew smaller and smaller, until it finally disappeared.

"We're alone," Hayley whispered.

Which wasn't really correct.

We were alone . . . but not for long. We were about to have a visitor—and it wasn't Ivan.

20

Hayley heard the noise at the exact same time I did. It didn't come from the corridor where Ivan had disappeared, but from ahead of us in the darkness.

At first, it was just a muffled sound, like a sweeping broom. Then it became louder and closer, and there was no mistaking what it was.

It was the sound of flapping wings.

The wings—of a bat.

Worse, I knew that it was a vampire bat, like Ivan had warned us about.

Suddenly, a dark shape swooped down on us. Hayley shrieked and flung herself to the floor, but she held onto the candle. I dropped to my knees and covered my head with my hands. The bat flew over our heads, screeching and screaming and flapping its wings.

And it was *enormous!* We have bats in Stowe, but they are small . . . about the size of a sparrow. The one that was attacking us was the size of a seagull!

I couldn't bear to think of how large its teeth would be.

"Ivan!" I screamed, hoping that he would hear me. *"There's a vampire bat after us!"*

Suddenly, the bat swooped down again, and this time I felt its wing clip my ear.

"Use the garlic!" Hayley cried. *"Use the garlic!"*

I fumbled in the dim light and opened the drawstring that knotted the leather bag closed. A garlic bulb fell out and I scooped it up. I wasn't sure what I was going to do with it. I guess I figured I would throw it at the bat, but I knew it was going to be difficult, since we could only see the creature when it flew right over our heads.

The bat spun at us again, but this time, it didn't flee. It circled above Hayley, madly flapping its wings. Hayley was terrified. She remained flat on the floor, face down, one hand covering the back of her head, the other still holding the flickering candle.

Then, the bat swerved . . . and attacked *me!* The creature came right at me, mouth open, teeth bared.

I threw my arm out in front of me to knock the creature away, but it was too late. The bat's mouth was open wide, and in the next moment he bit down . . . *right into the garlic bulb in my hand!*

Instantly, the bat squealed and shrieked. It flapped like crazy. It was as if it was actually stuck to the garlic, and couldn't get away.

I let go of the bulb and the bat fell to the floor, flopping wildly, the garlic still in its mouth.

Then, a really weird thing happened.

The bat began to glow!

As it flapped madly on the stone floor, it began to glow different colors. First yellow, then orange, then red, then yellow again.

And it began to shrink. Its wings got all wrinkly and began to curl up. In a few more seconds, the bat had shriveled up . . . and vanished. Only the garlic bulb remained.

Hayley was still on the stone floor, one hand over the back of her head.

"I can't believe that just happened," I panted.

"Is it safe?" Hayley asked.

"Yeah," I replied. "The bat is gone. At least, I *think* it is."

Hayley pulled her hand away from her head and propped herself up on her elbows, one hand still holding the lit candle. Her eyes were wide as she warily looked up and around, as if she might have to duck again at any moment.

I explained to her what happened, and how the bat had bitten into the garlic.

"It was just like Ivan said," I told her. "The garlic seemed to drain all of the energy from the bat, and it just shriveled up and disappeared."

I got up, and then I helped Hayley to her feet.

Still, there was no sign of Ivan.

"I hope he's okay," I said.

"What if he's not?" Hayley asked. "What if something happened to him, and we aren't there to help him?"

We were in a tough spot. Ivan had told us to wait here. But if something had happened and he needed our help . . . .

"Let's go look for him," I said. "Give me the candle."

Hayley handed me the candle. It felt warm and greasy in my hand. I knelt down, and with my free hand, I scooped up the garlic bulb that I'd used to stop the bat. I figured that I would carry the candle in one hand and the garlic bulb in the other, just in case I needed to use it in a hurry. Then I pulled the bag's drawstring tight, sealing it up so the rest of the garlic wouldn't fall out.

"I'll carry it," Hayley said, and she picked up the bag and slung it over her shoulder.

Slowly, we started walking in the direction we had last seen Ivan. I called out to him as we walked, but he didn't reply.

Finally, the corridor widened. It seemed like we were in some big room, but there wasn't enough candlelight to be able to tell for sure. The air was heavy and damp, and a bit chilly.

"Ivan?" I called out again, as Hayley and I made our way cautiously across the room. There were no tables, no chairs, no furniture of any sort. None that we could see, anyway. It was just a big, empty room.

"There's got to be another hallway somewhere," I said quietly. "All we have to do is find it."

"Where do you think Ivan went?" Hayley asked.

"I don't know," I said. "Remember, he told us that the inside of the castle changes every time you play the game . . . or enter the castle. I hope he didn't get lost in his own castle."

"When we get out of here, I'm never playing this game," Hayley said.

"Oh, I think it would be a fun game," I said. "But the computer is all messed up. All we need to do is—"

Hayley gasped, and I stopped speaking. She grasped my hand.

"What was that?!?!" she whispered frantically.

"What was what?" I asked. "I didn't hear anything."

I had no sooner said those words when I *did* hear something.

A growl.

Low and rumbling, slow and certain.

Snarling with fury and rage.

In the darkness, we couldn't see anything, but Hayley knew the same thing that I knew.

Somewhere in the room, not far from us, was a robotic wolf.

Fear gnawed at the depths of my belly. I was so terrified that I felt dizzy. I wanted to run, but I was paralyzed with terror.

Hayley was scared, too. She grabbed my arm and held it like a vice, squeezing so hard that it hurt.

"Is . . . is that what I think it is?" Hayley stammered quietly. Her voice quaked. "Is it one of those robotic wolves?"

"I'm not sure," I said. "Don't move. Remember: Ivan said that robotic wolves aren't like real wolves. They can't hear or smell as well as real animals."

I took a quiet breath and blew out the candle. If there really *was* a robotic wolf around, I didn't want him to see the glowing wick and come after us.

We heard another sound, like nails scratching on stone. Whatever it was, it wasn't very far away.

Suddenly, two red beams, each as thin as a pencil, glowed. They were like lasers, and they swept around the room.

"It's the wolf's eyes!" I whispered frantically. *"He's looking for us!"*

Although we couldn't see the creature, we could see where he was by looking at where the red beams originated. He was on the other side of the room, moving slowly away from us.

Which meant that he hadn't spotted us—yet. But I knew that if the wolf turned his head in our direction, he'd see us for sure.

Then, we'd be in a lot of trouble. Especially since the garlic didn't do anything to the wolf, and we didn't have any way to defend ourselves.

Slowly, the two red beams began to sway in our direction. I pulled Hayley to the stone floor, just as the two red lasers went over our heads. If we had been standing up at that moment, the robotic wolf would have spotted us.

We remained hunched down on the floor as the strange red beams continued their search, sweeping along the walls and the floor. Once again, we had to duck down as the lasers came close to us.

But the wolf didn't see us. We could hear him moving farther away, and I began to breathe easier. The wolf hadn't found us, and he would soon be gone.

And then I sneezed.

It happened so fast that I didn't even feel the sneeze coming on, or I would have tried to hold it in.

"Ah . . . CHOO!"

Suddenly, the two red beams were trained right on me. Hayley gasped and squeezed my arm—just as the wolf attacked.

The only thing we could see were two glaring, red eyes coming at us. The wolf was snarling, but its growls sounded mechanical, machine-like. Metal claws scraped stone.

In the darkness, Hayley and I dove to the side. We couldn't see where we were going, but one thing was certain: we wanted to get away from the wolf.

Suddenly, we heard another snarl and more frantic scraping of claws on stone. The wolf's red eyes darted away from us. Something had attracted its attention, and in the next instant, the wolf was locked in a fierce battle with another creature.

Hayley and I crawled on our hands and knees until we reached a wall. Then we turned to watch the bizarre sight.

And I'll say this: it was really weird, sitting on the cold stone floor, watching nothing but two red beams slashing through the darkness. We knew that the wolf was fighting something, but we couldn't see what it was. We could hear mechanical growls and snarls, along with what sounded like real animal snarls, but it was too dark to see anything else.

The fierce battle raged on for nearly a minute. Then, without any warning at all, the two red beams fled. We heard the wolf's claws scraping the stone floor as the creature ran out of the room. The sounds faded away, and the room was as black as night.

But we weren't alone. Somewhere in the large room was another animal. We could hear its claws scratching the floor as it walked. The sounds drew nearer, and, although I couldn't see anything, I knew that the creature was right in front of us.

I could hear Hayley's teeth chattering. My heart pounded so hard that I thought it was going to break my ribs.

And suddenly, a warm, moist tongue was on my cheek. The sensation surprised and scared me and I drew back . . . until I realized what it was.

A dog!

I laughed, and threw my arms around the big animal.

"It's okay!" I told Hayley as I scratched the dog's ears. "It's Zeena! Zeena saved us!"

I heard a match strike, and suddenly a tiny, yellow flare exploded to life. Zeena was sitting right in front of me, and, as Hayley re-lit her candle, the dog wagged its tail and sniffed the air.

I reached into my pocket, pulled out my candle, and touched it to the wick of Hayley's candle. I felt safer now, being that we had light to see . . . and a protective dog with us!

And then we heard something else:

A voice!

"There you are!" Ivan's voice called out. Another glowing candle appeared, and he entered the large room. "Man . . . I've been looking all over for you guys!"

"We thought something happened to you," I said, "so we went to look for you."

"I'm fine," Ivan replied. "After I left you, I decided that it might be better if Zeena was with us. I went to look for her. Thankfully, she was in the castle."

"You found her just in time," Hayley said with relief. "One of those weird robot wolves was just about to gobble us up!"

"But Zeena attacked, and the robotic wolf ran away," I said, patting the dog on her head. Zeena licked my hand.

"I'm sure glad I found you," Ivan said as he approached.

"So are we," I replied.

I stood up, then helped Hayley to her feet. When the wolf had attacked, she had dropped the bag of garlic. Now, she walked over to it and picked it up. I had dropped the garlic bulb I had been carrying and I reached down and retrieved it.

"It's a lot worse than what I thought," Ivan said grimly.

"What do you mean?" Hayley asked.

Ivan looked at Hayley, then at me. He drew a breath, and in the glow of the three candles, I could see the tips of his fangs at the corners of his mouth.

And when he told us what had happened, we knew that we finally had to face a cold, hard fact:

There was a good chance that we would *never* make it out of Virtuality.

Ever.

"The castle itself seems to be changing," he began. "I don't know how to explain it. But I think that whatever is creating the other vampires is also having an effect on the castle."

That made sense. "Well," I said, "if the vampires have been brought about by a virus or a malfunction in the computer, the problem could affect other things, too."

"I think that's what's happening," Ivan said with a nod. "But Virtuality seems to be running out of energy. Everything seems to be slowing down."

"But where is the energy coming from in the first place?" I asked. "When you pulled us out of our world, the computer wasn't even plugged into the wall."

"I don't know," Ivan said, "but the power source is coming from somewhere. Most importantly, there is another source of energy that the mutated vampires are interested in."

He stopped speaking. I didn't understand what he was saying, and I nodded curiously.

Then, Ivan pointed at me. And at Hayley.

"Both of you," he said. "You have enough energy to keep the virtual world running . . . at least for a little while. You two are the strongest sources of energy in Virtuality—and I'm sure the mutated vampires know this."

"But won't we run out of energy?" Hayley asked.

Ivan nodded. "Sooner or later, yes," he said. "But the mutated vampires aren't going to let that happen. They'll want to drain you of your energy before it's all gone, so they can leave Virtuality and travel to your world, where they will have an endless supply of energy. There's no telling what will happen in your world once that happens."

"So, we have to get into the computer and fix the problem before we run out of energy?" I asked.

Again, Ivan nodded. "And you have to do it without interference from any of the mutated vampires."

"But how much energy do we have?" Hayley asked. "When will we run out of energy?"

"I don't know," Ivan said, "but I do know this: we're using up a lot of energy just standing here and doing nothing. We've got to get moving, and find the dungeon and the passageway that leads into the machine. And we've got to do it before the vampires find you."

The task seemed impossible. Since we had no way of knowing just how to get to the dungeon, we could walk around for hours trying to find it. And the longer it took to find it, the more chance the vampires would have to find *us*.

"Let's get started," I said.

"Yeah," Hayley agreed.

"Come on," Ivan said. "Keep that garlic handy, but don't get it too close to me."

And it was at that very moment that Zeena began growling . . . .

Zeena's growls were ferocious. She even had *me* scared. I knew that she was a friendly dog, but I sure wouldn't want her mad at me.

Suddenly, Zeena stopped growling. She whimpered and then walked close to Ivan. It was obvious that she was afraid of something.

All too soon, we found out what it was.

On the floor, not six feet away, a shape was beginning to form. At first, it looked like a wisp of smoke. Then it grew thicker, like a blob. It was like it was materializing right out of thin air!

"Uh-oh," Ivan said, taking a step back. He held his candle out. "There is only one thing this could be."

Seeing Ivan step back caused Hayley and me to also step away from the shape that was appearing before us on the floor.

"What is it?" Hayley whispered.

"A deranged cat," Ivan said quietly. "Don't move. Stay as still as you can."

In the next moment, the cat appeared. It was all black, with glowing green eyes. It sat on the stone floor, watching us, its tail swishing back and forth like a wire.

"Why is Zeena afraid of a cat?" I whispered. It seemed strange that she could fight off a robotic wolf and be afraid of a small black cat.

"It's more than just a cat," Ivan replied quietly. *"It may look small, but the deranged cats in this castle are every bit as ferocious as a lion."*

I found that hard to believe. I've been around cats all my life, and I'd never heard of a cat acting like a lion.

But, then again, I'd never been to Virtuality before.

Just then, the cat opened its mouth. I thought the small animal was going to yawn, but that's not what it did. The room was suddenly filled with a deafening roar! It sounded *exactly* like a lion! We all jumped, and Zeena whimpered again.

I couldn't believe that such a big sound could come from such a small creature.

"Can . . . can we . . . run?" Hayley stammered.

"No," Ivan said, slowly shaking his head. "The cat will come after us for sure. And there's no way we can outrun it."

"So . . . what *do* we do?" I asked. "Just stand here and wait for it to attack?"

"Its hard to know just what it will do," Ivan said.

"Well, what would *you* do if we weren't here?" Hayley asked.

"It's not me the cat is interested in," Ivan said. "The cat senses your energy. It's *you two* that the cat is interested in."

"When you say 'interested'," Hayley said, "do you mean 'hungry'?"

Ivan drew in a breath. He was about to answer, but suddenly, the deranged cat turned its head. We watched as the cat peered into the darkness. It seemed to be alarmed by something.

Then, the cat drew back. It cocked its head, and, while we watched, the animal slowly began to vanish. In seconds, the cat was gone.

I let out a breath, and so did Hayley.

"Whew," I said. "I'm glad he's gone. If Zeena doesn't want to mess with a cat, I don't—"

Ivan touched my shoulder, and I stopped speaking. He was looking into the darkness, squinting. I followed his gaze, and so did Hayley.

We didn't see anything—yet.

But we were about to.

For the first time, we were about to have an encounter with a mutated vampire.

25

I strained to listen, but I didn't hear anything. Obviously, Ivan knew something that we didn't. He placed a finger to his lips, urging us to remain silent. Hayley squeezed my hand. In my other hand, I gripped the leather bag containing the garlic bulbs.

Have you ever felt like you were being watched, but couldn't tell just who—or what—was watching you? That's how I felt. And with every passing second, my fear grew.

And when the mutated vampire spoke, a chill went through my entire body.

"Ener . . . gee," the sinister voice hissed. *"Energy!"*

Still, we couldn't see the creature. Ivan was standing on my left with Zeena right beside him. Hayley was on my right, still carrying the bag of garlic.

I was still carrying a garlic bulb in my hand, and I squeezed it tightly. Then, emerging from the darkness, I saw one of the most horrifying things I have ever seen in my life.

It was a vampire . . . and worse. In a way, he looked a lot like you would expect a vampire to look. He was dressed all in black, and his skin was pasty-white and looked plastic, like he was some kind of oversized doll that hadn't been made quite right.

His arms were outstretched and he slowly came toward us. I heard Hayley gasp. Zeena backed away with a whimper. Even Ivan looked terrified.

"Energy," the vampire hissed, exposing two very long, very sharp fangs. *"Energy . . . ."*

"Mike . . . hold up your garlic," Ivan said quietly as he took a step away from me. I knew that he needed to be careful that he didn't get too close to the garlic himself.

The mutated vampire was still coming toward us. He looked awful. I mean, he really looked like he was sick or something. I've had bad nightmares before, but the vampire that was only a few feet in front of me was scarier than any creature of my imagination.

Suddenly, I thrust out my hand and held up the garlic bulb for the creature to see.

Instantly, the mutated vampire stopped. He raised his hands to shield his face, as if he was trying to protect himself from something. He opened his mouth wide and he hissed loudly. His eyes bulged with anger and fury.

I have to admit, I was really, really scared. I didn't know what the vampire would do.

Then, he took a step backward. And another. Then another. The more he stepped back, the braver I became. Ivan was right! The garlic really worked!

Still holding out the bulb, I stepped toward the retreating creature.

That was all it took. The mutated vampire suddenly spun sideways . . . and vanished into the darkness.

"You did it!" Hayley exclaimed from behind me. "You scared him away!"

"One down," I said confidently.

Ivan shook his head. "Not really," he said. "Oh, you scared him off, and you made him mad. But you didn't stop him. He's still here—along with more vampires—in the castle."

"Yeah, but if all I have to do is show them the garlic," I said, "we're home free. All we have to do is find the dungeon. Taking care of the mutated vampires is going to be a cinch."

115

Well, that's what I *said.*

That's what I *thought.*

I really believed that it would be a cinch to scare off the vampires.

But I was only moments away of finding out just how wrong I was.

We started moving again. Ivan was ahead of us, carrying his candle, followed by Hayley, and then me. Zeena walked at Ivan's side. We walked silently, and our shadows breezed along the stone walls and floor like black ghosts. With three lit candles, it was easier to see our surroundings. Not much, but three candles were certainly better than one.

Suddenly, we came to a dead end. The hallway just stopped at a brick wall.

"Where are we?" Hayley asked, looking around at the brick walls.

Ivan shook his head. "This is much worse than I thought," he said. "The castle is changing very fast. There aren't supposed to be any dead ends anywhere. We'll have to go back."

"Wait a minute," Hayley said. "Maybe it's not a dead end."

"What do you mean?" I asked.

"I saw a movie once about a hallway like this," she explained. "It *seemed* to end at a brick wall, but it was actually a false wall."

"A false wall?" Ivan asked.

Hayley nodded. "There was a hidden passageway on the other side of the wall."

"But in the movie, how did they find out?"

"They pushed on a brick," Hayley said. "Like this. Hold my candle."

I took the candle from her. Hayley placed the leather bag on the floor. Then she stepped toward the wall, placed her hands on a brick and pushed.

Nothing happened.

"So much for false walls," I said glumly.

"Well, in the movie, they didn't find it right away," Hayley said. She moved her hands to another brick, and pushed.

Nothing.

Then she went to another brick.

Still nothing.

"Come on," I said. "We're wasting time. We've got to—"

But my sentence was abruptly halted when a brick suddenly moved beneath Hayley's hands. She pushed harder . . . and a hole appeared in the wall as the brick fell. We heard the heavy brick tumble to the stone floor on the other side of the wall.

"Hayley, you're a *genius!*" I exclaimed.

"I knew it!" she said. "I knew that we'd find something like this. I'll bet more of these bricks will move, too!"

She was about to try another brick, but a swift motion from the hole in the wall stopped her.

Not only did it stop her, it *grabbed* her.

And when I saw what it was, I gasped. Hayley screamed.

Something had reached through the hole in the wall and grasped her wrists.

And that something . . . was a mutated vampire!

27

The scene was chaotic. I thought the mutated vampire was trying to pull Hayley through the hole in the wall. Which, of course, was impossible . . . Hayley was too big to fit. She was screaming and screeching and trying to pull away. Zeena was barking and growling furiously.

But then I realized that the vampire wasn't trying to pull Hayley through.

He was stealing her energy!

Ivan shrieked, confirming my suspicion.

"You've got to save her!" he exclaimed. "Use a garlic bulb before it's too late! Hurry!"

Ivan backed away, making sure he was a good distance from the bag of garlic that Hayley had placed on the floor. I placed both candles on the floor, then

I reached one hand into the bag and pulled out a round, solid bulb.

"What do I do?!?!" I asked Ivan.

"Just drop one of the garlic bulbs through the hole!" he replied. "Hurry! Before it's too late!"

Hayley had stopped screaming, but she was still struggling madly, her arms held tightly by the grip of the unseen vampire.

I stepped up to her. In one quick motion, I thrust the garlic bulb through the hole. It was difficult to do, because I had to push Hayley's arms out of the way. Plus, I was worried that the mutated vampire might grab *me*.

Without wasting any time, I let go of the garlic bulb and withdrew my hand.

Instantly, there was a flash of light from the square hole, along with a terrible wailing. Hayley was suddenly free, and she tumbled backward and almost fell. I leapt back.

The terrible screeching on the other side of the wall continued. Bright, multicolored lights flashed from the rectangular opening, exploding like fireworks.

After a few moments, the screaming fell silent. The flashing lights dimmed, and then stopped. The only light was from the single candle that Ivan carried.

"That's how you take care of a mutated vampire," Ivan said, and he stepped up to the hole in the wall where the brick had been. He held up the candle and cocked his head curiously around, peering through the hole in the wall.

Suddenly, he gasped.

"Oh my gosh!" he exclaimed. *"You're not going to believe what's on the other side of this wall!"*

28

Hayley and I hurried to Ivan's side. Zeena sat on the floor watching us. Ivan took a step back so Hayley and I could peer through the opening in the wall.

It was hard to see with only the single, tiny candle flame, but I could make out the garlic bulb on the stone floor. There was no sign of the mutated vampire that had attacked Hayley. But I could see another corridor . . . with steps leading down!

"The dungeon!" I exclaimed. "Do you think those steps lead there?!?!"

"I think so," Ivan replied. "I can't be sure, though. Let's see if we can move any more of these bricks."

Sure enough, several other bricks came out. Some of them came away easy, others were stubborn and took all three of us to remove. Soon, we had pulled away enough bricks to create a small opening.

"Zeena!" Ivan called.

Instantly, Zeena bounded to her feet and slipped through the hole we'd created by pushing away the bricks. She walked cautiously along the corridor, sniffing the floor. When she reached the stairs leading down, she stopped, raised her head, and sniffed the air. Then she barked once.

"Good girl!" Ivan called out.

"That's a smart dog," Hayley said.

With a candle in one hand, Ivan knelt down and scrambled through the hole. He turned and held the candle up so we could see. Hayley picked up her candle, then climbed through the opening. Likewise, I picked up my candle, along with the bag of garlic, and followed.

The hallway we were now in looked identical to the one we had just left. However, a few feet away, stone steps plunged down into darkness. Immediately to the right of us, another dark hallway led to who knows where.

"That's probably where the mutated vampire came from," Ivan said, holding his candle up. "He probably came in from that hall."

"Well, now we know where *not* to go," I said.

Zeena still stood at the top of the steps, and the three of us walked up to her and stopped. In the murky light, we could see the steps leading down . . . to a door!

"That's it!" Ivan exclaimed. "It has to be!"

He bounded down the steps with Zeena at his heels. Hayley and I followed.

The door at the bottom of the steps was made of wood, and it was very solid. There was no window or opening to see through. In the middle of the door, on the left, was a large, iron handle.

"Here," Ivan said, handing me the candle. "Hold this."

I took the candle from him and held it up in the air, hoping to give him as much light as possible.

Ivan reached out, grasped the handle, and pulled. The door began to open, and Hayley and I stepped back to give Ivan more room.

Cautiously, Ivan opened the door a tiny bit. Then he leaned up to the crack and peered through.

"We're here!" he said, as he flung the door all the way open. "We found the dungeon!"

"How do you know for sure?" I asked. "If the castle is changing all the time, how do you know this is really the dungeon?"

"Look on the floor," Ivan replied, nodding down. "That's the goop I was telling you about. It's very, very dangerous."

Sure enough, the floor was covered with a strange, gelatin-like substance. It looked shiny and slimy and wet, and, from where I stood, it appeared to be several inches deep.

But the dungeon wasn't very big . . . maybe the size of my bedroom. And on the other side—

A door!

But it wasn't like any door I had ever seen. Instead of being made of a solid substance like wood or metal, the door appeared to be watery, like a sheen of clear plastic. It shimmered and wavered, creating fine ripples on its surface.

Ivan motioned toward the far side of the dungeon. "That's the virtual door that leads into the machine," he said. "You don't have to open it . . . all you have to do is step through."

"But how are we going to get to it?" Hayley asked. "I mean . . . if that goop is as dangerous as you say it is, how are we going to get to the other side of the dungeon?"

Now *that* was a problem. Somehow, we had to get to the door on the other side of the dungeon . . . without touching the goop. It seemed impossible.

The three of us stood silently, looking and thinking, trying to figure out how we could make it across the dungeon.

"Maybe we could take this door off its hinges," I suggested. "We could use the wood and make a bridge to walk on."

"That's a good idea," Ivan said, stepping back and inspecting the door. "But the door is heavy. We'd never get it off its hinges unless we had some tools. And even if we did, it's still not long enough for us to reach the other side of the dungeon."

Just then, Zeena began growling. We turned to see her looking up the stone stairs.

"What is it, girl?" Ivan said.

I didn't want to find out. We'd already had enough trouble, and we didn't need anymore.

"Get a garlic bulb," Ivan ordered. "Be ready, just in case."

I placed the bag on the floor, reached into it, and pulled out a garlic bulb.

Zeena was still staring up, hackles raised, growling. But there was nothing there—at least, not at the moment.

We watched in silence. Zeena's growls were soft and low. Menacing.

And suddenly, there *was* something there. Something small seemed to be materializing at the top of the steps.

"It's a deranged cat," Ivan whispered. *"It has to be."*

And that's exactly what it was. In the next instant the cat was fully visible, standing at the top of the stairs, staring down at us. Zeena shuffled nervously. She knew she was no match for a deranged cat.

Suddenly, the cat let out a roar that sounded like thunder! It was really strange, looking at what appeared to be an ordinary, black house cat, yet hearing it roar like a charging lion.

But the sudden, loud roar was too much for Zeena. The dog jumped in fright, spun around, and ran smack into Hayley . . . knocking her backwards, tumbling and flailing into the dungeon . . . and into the terrible, sticky goop on the floor.

Hayley didn't even have time to scream. One moment she was standing next to me, and, in the next, she was falling into the sticky, oozing goop. Her candle was knocked out of her hand, and it went out when it hit the floor.

However, just before her whole body fell into the gooey mass, she was able to break her fall with her hands . . . which plunged right into the gooey jelly.

Then she *did* scream. When she realized that her hands were covered with the awful goop, she knew that she was in a lot of trouble. After all, Ivan said that the strange liquid had eaten into his shoes. I didn't even want to *think* about what it could do to human skin.

If there was any good news, it was the fact that the deranged cat was gone. I had no idea where he went, but the creature was no longer at the top of the steps.

I reached down and grabbed Hayley's arm to pull her out, and, as I did, I got some of the goop onto my hand. But I ignored it, and grabbed Hayley's arm and pulled her up and back through the door.

She stood up. Jelly-like goop was all over her hands. A little bit of it had splashed onto her face.

And I still had it on my hand, too!

Ivan looked at us, horrified.

"Does . . . does it hurt?" he asked.

"Actually, no," I said, holding the candle close and staring curiously at the gelatin on my hand and wrist. "It doesn't hurt at all. It feels sticky, but it doesn't hurt."

I raised my hand to my nose. "Wait a minute," I said with a sniff. "I know what this is!"

"You do?" Hayley replied. She looked relieved. We were both glad that the goop had turned out to be harmless.

I laughed. "This is soda pop! I'd know that smell anywhere!"

Hayley raised a goop-covered hand to her nose and gave a sniff.

"You're right!" she cried, happy that the goop wasn't eating away at her skin. "It's just gooey soda pop!"

"This is what happens to soda pop if it gets spilled and it isn't cleaned up," I explained to Ivan. "It gets real thick and sticky."

"I don't understand," Ivan said.

"I'm not sure I do, either," I said to Ivan. "But I'll bet that, since you're a virtual being, you react differently to the soda pop. However, Hayley and I are from the real world, so soda pop doesn't hurt us at all."

Ivan nodded. He seemed to understand—and that was mystery solved.

"The computer is malfunctioning because somebody spilled soda pop all over it!" I blurted out, snapping my fingers. "I'll bet that's what's causing the problems!"

Hayley's eyes went wide. "Mike! You're right!" she exclaimed. "I'll bet that's what's been causing all of the problems in Virtuality!"

"Well, maybe not all of the problems," I said. "But it makes sense that the spilled soda pop would only add to the problems."

"Do you think you can fix it?" Ivan asked.

"I hope so," I answered. "I really do. All we need to do is get into the computer and see what damage has been done. Hopefully, not too much."

"The machine is on the other side of that virtual door," Ivan said, pointing across the dungeon. "But I won't be able to go with you."

"That's okay," I said. "You can stay here with Zeena. Hayley and I can walk through the goop and through the virtual door. We'll see if we can fix the computer from the inside."

At last, things were going our way. I really felt hopeful, and I knew that we were going to be able to get out of Virtuality and go back home. I just *knew* it. I wasn't quite sure what to expect on the other side of the virtual door, but I assumed that it would be the inside of the computer. We would get into the computer, fix the problem, and finally be able to go home. Ivan would have his castle back, and be safe from the mutating vampires.

But there was something we hadn't counted on.

Something that we hadn't thought about.

Something that was waiting for us . . . *inside the computer!*

30

This is what we decided to do:

Hayley and I would go through the dungeon and pass through the virtual door. Then we would actually be *inside* my computer.

Which is really weird, when you think about it. That would mean that Hayley and I would be very, very tiny. Perhaps even smaller than a mouse.

Hopefully, a lot of the problems in Virtuality were caused by the spilled soda pop. If we could clean up the mess, maybe we could get the computer working better. We'd worry about any computer viruses later.

At least, that's what I was hoping to do. I knew that our time was running out, and we would have to act fast.

"Zeena and I will stay here and make sure that no mutated vampires come along," he said.

"Yeah, and try to keep those creepy bats and cats and wolves away, too," Hayley said.

"I'll do what I can. Do you really think that you can fix the machine and make things in Virtuality normal again?" He had a worried look on his face, and I knew that he was really concerned. After all, this was his home. If we couldn't get the computer fixed, he, too, had a lot to lose.

"I think I can," I assured him. "I really do."

And with that, we stepped into the dark dungeon. The gooey soda pop stuck to my tennis shoes. It was like walking in gum.

We approached the virtual door. As we drew closer, we could hear it buzzing, like electricity. It continued to shimmer and shine.

"Go ahead," Ivan called out from behind us. "You'll be okay. Just step through."

I closed my eyes and took a giant step forward. Hayley followed. I opened my eyes.

"Wow," I whispered. *"Look at that."*

Hayley held up her candle and peered over my shoulder.

"Wow," Hayley echoed. Both of us just stared.

The virtual door was now behind us. From where we stood, I saw exactly what I had expected: the inside of the computer. There were wires and capacitors and all sorts of electrical components. Of course, I'd seen all of this before, but never this close. The wires were big, like cables. Everything appeared to be huge.

And another thing that I noticed:

The computer seemed to be off. When we were pulled into Virtuality, the computer had been on, even though it was unplugged. Now, however, there was nothing to be heard.

"Man, I wonder what Mom would do if she saw me now," I said. "I bet we're only an inch tall!"

"I wonder what my cat would do," Hayley said.

I laughed nervously. That was a pretty funny—and *scary*—thought.

Ivan's voice echoed across the small dungeon. His voice sounded oddly electronic through the virtual door. "What do you see?" he asked.

"It's the computer, alright," I replied loudly. "It's just like you said. The virtual door leads right into the computer."

I lowered the candle and looked down. There was brown goop all over the place, covering wires and everything.

"We've got to get to work cleaning this up," Hayley said.

Which was going to be a pretty tough job. We didn't have any cleaning supplies or any rags.

"I know!" Hayley said. She turned around and looked across the dungeon. Ivan was still standing on the other side, holding a candle.

"Ivan!" she said. "Can we use your cape?"

"I guess so," Ivan replied, and he reached behind his head and began to pull off his cape. "What for?"

"We can use it to wipe up a lot of this gunk," Hayley said, walking back through the dungeon. Her shoes made a curious, squeaky sound as she made her way through the goop. "I'm afraid it will be ruined, though," she said.

"That's okay," Ivan said, handing her the black cape. "If you can make things right in Virtuality again, it will be worth it."

Hayley walked back to where I stood. "Let's get to work," she said.

We placed our candles on a piece of metal that served as a shelf. Then Hayley tore the cape right down the middle and gave me one of the cloths.

Cleaning up the goop was really difficult. It was everywhere, and it was really sticky and messy. We wiped off wires and buttons, and anything that was coated with the brownish, filmy goop.

Finally, we had most of the spilled soda pop cleaned up. There still was a lot of it beneath our feet, but, since it wasn't touching any important parts of the computer, I didn't think it would hurt anything. Besides . . . I knew we were running out of time.

I picked up my candle and walked a few steps back to the door. Ivan and Zeena were still standing guard on the other side of the dungeon.

"I think we've got the problem fixed," I said. "Hayley and I have to go farther into the computer and make sure there isn't any more spilled soda pop. We'll be back as fast as we can."

"Good luck," Ivan said.

We were going to need it.

"At least we won't have to worry about vampires, robotic wolves and cats that appear out of thin air," Hayley said with a sigh.

And she was right.

Unfortunately, we had something a lot *worse* to worry about.

Because a giant, menacing worm was lurking in the computer . . . and he was about to find us.

We both carried our lit candles. As we made our way around the maze of electrical components and wires. I recognized the computer's hard drive, and the machine's processor. It sure was strange, being so small like we were! Everything appeared to be gigantic.

We had to be careful. We had to climb up and over wires and other electrical parts while carrying our candles. I didn't want to accidentally drip wax on any of the components, or, even worse, catch something on fire.

Thankfully, we didn't find any more spilled soda pop. There was a lot of dust everywhere, but we didn't see anything else that might cause the computer to screw up.

"I think everything's okay," I said. "Let's head back and ask Ivan what we need to do next."

I was about to turn around when I noticed something on one of the large electrical panels.

"Wait a minute," I said, holding my candle out.

"What is it?" Hayley asked.

"That!" I said, pointing to a tangled maze of wires. A green wire had become detached from the panel, and I could see where it had broken off. *"There's another problem, right there!"* I exclaimed.

"I thought that the spilled soda pop was causing all the problems," Hayley said.

"The spilled soda pop was probably causing the computer to run slow," I said. "That green wire is supposed to be connected to that panel. I'll bet the computer won't work right with that wire disconnected."

"Can you fix it?" Hayley asked.

"Yeah," I said. "I think I can. Here . . . hold my candle."

Hayley took my candle, and she held both of them out so I could see better.

The green wire was wrapped in a bundle containing several other wires. I would have to climb over a silver box, slide next to the hard drive, reach out, and reconnect the wire to the panel.

I had just started to move when a noise from behind me caught my attention. At first, I thought it was Hayley.

And then I heard her scream . . . and I knew that we weren't alone in the computer.

Hayley's scream was loud and shrill. It surprised me so much that I almost dropped my candle.

But when I turned and saw what had caused her to cry out, I felt like screaming, too.

A computer worm was squirming its way right toward us!

I had forgotten all about the worms that had attacked us on our way to Transylvania. Now, there was one right inside the computer . . . and he was headed right for us!

Hayley scrambled aside, still screaming.

"Mike! Do something! Do something!"

"I can't fight him off!" I shouted. *"He's ten times our size!"*

And he was getting closer and closer with each passing second.

Suddenly, I realized something.

If the faulty wire connection was causing the problems in Virtuality, then maybe if I could reconnect the wire, the problems would disappear . . . including the worm!

"Hang on!" I shouted, scrambling toward the wire. I grabbed it with my hand.

"Mike! He's getting closer! He's coming after us!"

I could hear the worm sliding through the gadgetry. It was a weird sound, like squishy muck.

Concentrating on the large, green wire, I pulled and twisted until the bare end of it connected to the panel. I wrapped the bare copper fibers around the connection post.

There was a single *pop!* followed by a click . . . and then:

Silence.

But most importantly, when I turned around, the worm was gone!

Hayley was still holding her candle, looking around in shock and disbelief.

"The worm!" she exclaimed. *"It vanished!"*

We looked around at all of the components surrounding us.

"I think that broken wire was the problem all along!" I exclaimed.

"And we found it just in time, too," Hayley added. "That giant worm was about to have us for lunch!"

"Let's go find Ivan," I said, making my way back to Hayley. "Now that things are fixed, he can show us how to get out of Virtuality and back to our world!"

We hurried as fast as we could in the dim light of the two candles, making our way back through the computer, around wires and gadgets and metal panels and components. Ahead of us, I could see the door that opened into the dungeon.

But when we reached it, Hayley and I suddenly realized we had another problem to deal with . . . .

33

We stopped and looked around. Our candles provided the only light, and the components around us wavered eerily in the flickering glow.

"Now what?" Hayley asked.

"We ask Ivan," I said. "He'll know what to do. Come on."

We walked to the door that led into the dungeon.

"Ivan?" I called out. "I think there's still a problem with the computer."

No answer.

"Ivan?"

Still no answer.

I stepped into the dungeon with Hayley right behind me. The sticky goop stuck to my shoes as I walked.

"Ivan?" I called out again, louder this time. "Zeena?"

Still, there was no response, and by the time we made it to the other side of the dungeon, it was obvious that Ivan and Zeena were gone.

"Maybe something happened to them when the computer started up," Hayley said.

Now *that* was a scary thought. If we'd done something to make Ivan vanish, then how would we ever get out of Virtuality?

Still, I wasn't ready to give up. I was sure that there had to be a way out.

We just had to figure out what it was.

"Maybe we should go and look for him," Hayley suggested.

I shook my head. "We could, but we can't risk getting lost in the castle and not finding our way back. And besides . . . if it turns out that we didn't fix the computer, that would mean that there are still mutated vampires and robotic wolves and deranged cats out there somewhere. And maybe even more computer worms."

"Well, we have to do *something,*" Hayley insisted. "Soon, our candles will be out, and we won't be able to see anything."

Hayley was right. Our candles had been burning a long time, and both of them were close to being used up. If the candles burned out, we'd have no light at all.

"It's too bad we can't just press a button and turn the computer on," Hayley said dejectedly.

Wait a minute, I thought. *Press a button?*

"Hayley, you're right!" I exclaimed.

"I am?" Hayley replied. "About what?"

"A button!" I exclaimed. "The computer has a power button on the outside . . . but that button activates a button on the *inside!* The computer isn't broken anymore! Now that we cleaned up the spilled soda pop and fixed that wire, it did exactly what it was supposed to do!"

"What's that?" Hayley asked.

"It shut itself down! We need to go back into the computer, find that button, and start it back up again!"

"But our candles are almost gone," Hayley said. "What happens if we get back inside the computer and we don't have any light?"

"That's a chance we'll have to take. Let's go."

We had no other options. We were headed back into the computer, just Hayley and me, and two rapidly diminishing candles.

And if we failed this time, we wouldn't ever make it out of Virtuality.

We talked as we made our way back across the dungeon, and into the computer.

"I think that's what Ivan meant," I said. "I think that once the computer is working right, then there will be enough power generated to send us out of Virtuality and back to our world."

"But how do we do it?" Hayley wondered aloud. "I mean . . . let's say we get the computer turned on. What do we do then? Is there some special place, or some special door that we go through?"

I certainly didn't have any answers. But I knew that we had to do *something*. We couldn't just hang around and wait for our candles to burn out.

"Do you know where the power button is?" Hayley asked.

"It's up near the top of the computer," I said. "We'll have to climb up over the hard drive and around a bunch of wires and microchips."

As we wound around and through the components, I noticed that my hand was getting warmer. My candle had burned down, and there was only a stub of wax left. It would only be a few minutes before it burned out. Hayley's candle was about to burn out, too.

When we reached the computer's hard drive, I climbed up on top of it. Then I reached down and helped Hayley up. Again, it was really weird to think that we were actually *inside* my computer.

I turned. At the far end of the hard drive, connected to the mainframe, I saw the power button. In real life, the button was only about a half an inch in diameter. But, being that we were so small, the button appeared to be the size of a garbage can!

"Ouch!" Hayley said. She dropped her candle and it bounced on the metal case of the hard drive. The wick flickered and went out. "I couldn't hold onto it any longer," she said. "It was starting to burn my fingers."

I stepped on the small stub of wax to make sure the candle was out. My candle was about to burn itself out, too. Carefully, I placed it on the hard drive.

"There," I said. "Now we'll have a little bit of light, at least for a few more minutes."

I dashed over to the main power button, and pushed it with both hands. It wouldn't budge.

"Hayley!" I said, and without another word, she joined me at the power button. We both leaned into it, pushing with all of our weight and all of our strength.

"I . . . I didn't . . . didn't think it would be this . . . this . . . hard," I stammered, as we struggled with the button.

Suddenly, the button moved. There was a loud click. Hayley and I stepped back, our breaths heaving.

The candle had finally burned down, and it flickered out. We were in total, complete darkness. I couldn't even see Hayley, and I knew she was right next to me!

There was another click, and then a whirring sound. Beneath us, the hard drive began to vibrate.

"We did it!" I said. *"We turned on the computer!"*

In the darkness, things began to hum and come to life. It was like I could actually *feel* the power going through the computer, activating microchips and processors and the hard drive.

But then, something else started to happen, and when I realized what it was, I knew it was already too late . . . .

The inside of a computer can be dangerous, simply because of all of the electricity moving through everything. That's why you never should take apart a computer when it's turned on or plugged into the wall. There's a danger of getting shocked . . . or worse.

And here we were, inside the computer, with electricity swirling all around us!

Worse, I could feel the electricity in the air. It gave my skin a really weird tingling feeling. My hair felt like it was standing on end.

"What's . . . what's happening?" Hayley stammered, her voice filled with fear.

"I think it's the electricity!" I said loudly, as more and more parts of the computer began to start up. "We've got to get out of here!"

"How?!?!" Hayley cried. "It's so dark, we can't see a thing! What if we touch something that has electricity going through it?!?!"

Hayley was right. While it was dangerous to be standing where we were, it might be a lot more dangerous trying to make our way through the computer in pitch darkness.

"Wait a minute!" Hayley exclaimed.

"What?" I said.

Suddenly, a tiny yellow flare glowed.

"I have the matches that the guy at the market gave me! I have a couple dozen left! We can use them to give us light to find our way back! When each match burns out, I'll light another one!"

"Let's go!" I exclaimed.

Hayley, holding the match out in front of her, led the way. We wound our way back through the maze of whirring fans and machines, climbing down through wires and microchips. As each match burned out, Hayley lit another one.

"How many matches do you have left?" I asked.

"Six, I think," Hayley said.

"I think the door to the dungeon is up ahead, on the other side of that tangle of wires," I said.

We continued on, careful not to touch anything that might be surging with electricity. Finally, the virtual door to the dungeon appeared before us, all glimmering and wavering.

"We made it," Hayley said, as she stepped out of the computer and into the dungeon.

I was right behind her . . . but the moment I passed through the virtual door and left the computer behind me, something really weird happened.

I felt really dizzy, like I was going to fall over. I reached out to grab Hayley but I missed.

Then I was spinning. My whole body felt really tight and squeezed, and I just knew that something awful was happening. My whole body started to glow, and I wondered if it had anything to do with the electricity.

And then—

Everything went black, and I fainted.

Suddenly, I came to. I was still standing, but I was disoriented and confused. Hayley was standing next to me.

And in the next moment, we realized where we were:

My room!

We were standing in front of my desk. The computer was on, and I could see *Return of the Vampire* on the monitor. The game was already running, waiting to be played.

"Did . . . did that just happen to us?" I asked.

Hayley nodded. "I think so," she said.

"Then we did it," I said, heaving a sigh of relief. "We fixed Virtuality by fixing the computer."

"I can't believe we made it out of there," Hayley said. "Actually, I can't believe it even happened in the first place. Wait until I tell my mom and dad! They'll never believe me!"

I shook my head. "Mine won't either," I said.

We both stared at the computer monitor. We could see Ivan's castle in the background, and the words *Play* and *Exit* on the screen.

"I don't think I'm going to play this for a while," I said, and I reached down and placed my hand on the mouse. I dragged the cursor over the *Exit* button, and clicked.

Nothing happened.

I clicked again.

Still, nothing happened.

"What's wrong?" Hayley asked.

"I don't know," I said, clicking again and again. "I think the computer froze up."

All at once, the screen went blank. The castle disappeared, and so did the *Play* and *Exit* icons.

"Uh-oh," I said. "Maybe we didn't fix the computer, after all."

Suddenly, to our horror, a face appeared on the screen . . . and it wasn't Ivan.

It was the face of a mutated vampire. He was smiling, and I could see two sharp, pointed teeth on each side of his mouth.

But when his hand reached through the monitor and grabbed my wrist, I knew that the nightmare hadn't ended.

It was just beginning.

37

Hayley shrieked and jumped back. I tried to pull away from the vampire, but his grip was too strong.

"Energy!" the vampire hissed. *"Energy! Energy!"*

"Let me go!" I screamed, struggling to break free. *"Let . . . me . . . GO!"*

I twisted my arm and pulled, but the vampire held fast.

Suddenly, another arm came through the screen, and I tried to dash to the side so it couldn't grab my free arm.

However, the arm didn't try to grab my arm. It grabbed the vampire's arm, and pulled! I was able to break free, and I leapt away from the computer.

Then, the horrifying face on the computer was gone, and replaced by—

Ivan!

"Guys!" he said frantically. *"Something's wrong! There's not much energy left in Virtuality! Something is wrong! Virtuality needs more power, and then the mutated vampires will be destroyed!"*

"But . . . but I thought that we fixed it!" I exclaimed. "We turned the computer on from the inside! That should have fixed the problem!"

"Wait!" Hayley exclaimed. "The power cord! Remember, when we were pulled into Virtuality, the cord wasn't plugged into the wall! It's probably still unplugged!"

I dashed over to the computer and leaned over my desk.

The cord was still unplugged!

I fell to my knees, grabbed the cord, and plugged it into the wall. Then I jumped up and bolted back to where Hayley was standing on the other side of the room. I wasn't going to take any chances.

The computer immediately began to re-start. The monitor brightened, and, after a few moments, the icons on my desktop appeared.

Along with a *new* icon.

An icon that read *Return of the Vampire*.

Hayley and I said nothing. We simply stood where we were, watching and waiting. When nothing happened after a few moments, I spoke.

"I've got to know," I said, and I walked toward the computer.

Hayley shook her head. "I don't think it's a good idea," she said.

"But we've got to find out," I said. "I've got to know if Ivan is okay."

Reluctantly, Hayley walked up to my side. "Okay," she said. "Let's see what happens."

I reached down, grasped the mouse gently, and brought the cursor over the *Return of the Vampire* icon.

I clicked.

Suddenly, the game started again. In a moment, Ivan's familiar castle was in view, along with the words *Play* and *Exit.*

I dragged the mouse and moved the cursor over the *Play* icon. The screen went blank . . . but only for a moment. Then, a series of instructions appeared.

And when I read the instructions, I could only gasp. I couldn't believe what I was reading.

38

I read the instructions out loud.

"Mike and Hayley are trapped in Virtuality, a land where terror awaits at every turn. Mutated vampires, robotic wolves, deranged cats, and vicious worms can appear anytime, anywhere."

Hayley gasped. "The game!" she exclaimed. "We're a part of the game!"

I continued reading. *"Ivan is a good vampire who lives in a castle in Transylvania. The player of the game must help Mike and Hayley—with the help of Ivan, and his dog, Zeena—save Virtuality and make their way through the castle and back to their world. Beware . . . horror lurks at every turn!"*

Hayley and I could only stare. We had become an actual part of the game!

169

"One thing is for sure," I said. "What we went through was no *game*. It was *real*."

"This is just too bizarre," I said.

When we finished reading all of the instructions, I clicked on the *Exit* button. Then I got down on my hands and knees.

"What are you doing?" asked Hayley.

"I'm looking for the virtual door," I answered. "Just in case. Remember . . . we entered into my computer through that door in the dungeon. I just want to see if there is a door from our world back into Virtuality."

I searched the entire unit, but I didn't find anything that looked like the door we had passed through. Finally, I stood up.

"How did that happen?" Hayley asked. "How did we become an actual part of the game?"

"I have no idea," I replied, shaking my head. "But at least the computer is fixed, and the game seems to be working right. I still don't understand how the computer worked with the power cord unplugged, though."

"Are you ever going to play the game?" Hayley asked.

"Yeah, I will," I said. "But not today. I've had enough of vampires for one day."

"Me, too," she said, breathing a sigh of relief. "But I wish we could talk to Ivan some more. He might be able to explain things a little better."

And it was that very moment that both of us each felt a cold hand around the back of our necks . . . .

I about jumped right out of my clothing!

Hayley shrieked, and I spun.

"Hey, hey, sorry about that," Dad said. "I didn't mean to scare you guys."

What a relief! It was only Dad!

"Man, you scared us!" I said. "We thought you were a vampire!"

"A vampire, hmmm?" he said with a smirk. "I think you've been watching too much television. How are you, Hayley?"

"Fine," Hayley replied.

"Dad . . . about this computer. Is there any way that it can work without being plugged into the wall?"

"Sure," Dad replied. "Last year, I took it apart and put in a battery back-up. That way, if I was working on the computer and there was a power failure, the computer wouldn't shut down right away. It would operate for about an hour on the battery. But I think I messed it up."

I looked at Hayley, then back up at Dad. "What do you mean?" I asked.

"Well," Dad replied with a grimace, "while I was installing the battery back-up, I spilled soda pop all over the inside of the computer. And I think I broke a wire or two. It never worked very well after that. Plus, it was getting old, so I got a new one and gave this one to you."

So that was it! There was a battery back-up in the computer all along!

I started laughing, and so did Hayley.

"What's so funny?" Dad asked.

"You wouldn't believe me if I told you," I said.

Hayley went home. I promised her that I wouldn't play the vampire game without her.

But neither one of us were ready to play the game quite yet. I had a feeling that we had been really lucky, and I wasn't ready to go through an experience like that again . . . even if it was only a game.

Several weeks passed. It snowed a lot, which was really cool. I love snow, and I couldn't wait to go to Mt. Mansfield and snowboard with my friends.

Which is where I met two kids from California. Melanie Doyle, and her brother, Cameron. They came to Stowe to visit their aunt for a week.

It was Saturday, and I was at Stowe Mountain Resort on Mt. Mansfield, on my favorite slope: Tyro Terrain Park. It has quarter pipes, gap jumps, rail slides, and a lot more. The snow was coming down like crazy, and there were a lot of people everywhere.

I was part way down the slope when I looked up and saw a huge shadow. I stopped and raised my hand above my eyes to shield them from the heavy falling snow.

It was a bald eagle! We have them here in Vermont, and we see them once in a while. But this one was flying really low, and I could see it real good. It was awesome. Bald eagles are gigantic.

Just then, two snowboarders—a boy and a girl—slid up to me and stopped. They, too, saw the eagle.

"Pretty cool, huh?" I said.

"Yeah," the girl said. "But I freaked out for a minute. I thought it was a condor."

175

I shook my head. "We don't have any condors in Vermont, I don't think," I said.

"Well, we have them in California. They're huge. Twice the size of eagles. In fact, my brother and I had an experience with condors that we'll never forget."

"Really?" I said. I'd heard about California Condors, but I didn't know much about them. I've certainly never seen any in Vermont!

"Yeah," said Cameron. He pointed into the sky and shook his head. "But you don't want to mess around with the condors that we ran into."

"Why?" I asked.

"You wouldn't believe us if we told you," Melanie replied, shaking her head.

Then I thought about what Hayley and I went through in Virtuality. We tried to explain it to some friends at school, but no one believed us.

"I've had some pretty bizarre things happen to me," I said, "so if you tell me what happened, I'll believe you. Promise."

The pair looked at one another.

"All right," Melanie said. "We'll tell you. Let's go down to the lodge and get some hot chocolate."

We snowboarded the rest of the way down Tyro Terrain Park. On the way, I thought about what Melanie and Cameron had told me, and I knew that it couldn't be any freakier than what had happened to Hayley and me.

But when we sat down in the lodge with our hot chocolate and they began to explain their story, I realized that what had happened to them was every bit as horrifying as the nightmare Hayley and I had been through . . . .

Next:

#14: Creepy Condors of California

Continue on for a FREE preview!

"Okay, Class," Mrs. Kramer said to everyone on the bus, "while we're visiting the Los Angeles Zoo, I want everyone to be on their best behavior. And remember: we all stick together as a group. Does anyone have any questions?"

We all shook our heads.

"All right, then," Mrs. Kramer said as the bus driver opened the door. "Let's have fun!"

All of my classmates let out a cheer, and we leapt to our feet. Our teacher, Mrs. Kramer, had arranged for a field trip to the Los Angeles Zoo. I had never been there before, and I was really excited. I was so excited that I had a hard time falling asleep last night.

"Isn't this cool, Melanie?" my friend Sara asked as we stepped off the bus. The day was sunny and hot. Just about *every* day is sunny and hot in southern California, but I was glad to finally get out of that stuffy bus.

"I can't wait!" I exclaimed. "I've never been here before!"

There are a ton of animals to see at the zoo, but our class was more interested in a bird. Not just *any* bird, either. A California condor. We'd been studying them in class, and we learned that the California condor is the largest flying bird in North America. It has a wingspan of over *nine feet!* We learned a lot about them, and how they almost became extinct. They're very rare, too. There are only about 200 of them left in the wild, and the rest are in zoos or research facilities. There are a few organizations that are working to help more California condors survive in the wild.

And today, we were going to see a real, live California condor, up close. Everyone in my class was really excited, including Mrs. Kramer.

We walked in a group to the zoo entrance. In minutes, we were inside. Mrs. Kramer was in front of us, and she stopped and turned.

"Does anyone know the name of the place where the birds are kept?" she asked. A few students raised their hands, but I was faster.

"Yes, Miss Doyle?"

"An aviary," I said. I knew this because my uncle used to work at an aviary, taking care of birds.

"Very good," Mrs. Kramer said. "Now, before we get to the aviary, I'd like to remind everyone to keep their hands outside of the cage. We don't want to disturb any of the birds."

We continued on, making our way past alligators, kangaroos, a big horn sheep . . . even a giraffe and an elephant! There sure are a lot of animals at the Los Angeles Zoo.

Finally, we came to the aviary, and when we saw the enormous condor perched on a large tree branch, we all gasped. The bird was *enormous* . . . bigger than I'd even imagined. It was almost all black. Most of the birds' head and neck were completely bare, except for a couple of feathers. Its head was a mix of different colors: blue, yellow, and red, mostly.

And not to be mean . . . but California condors aren't the prettiest birds you'll ever see. If fact, I thought that the one at the Los Angeles Zoo looked a bit scary.

But now, when I look back at that day and remember my field trip, I had no way of knowing that condors could not only be scary—they could be *horrifying*.

Terrifying.

Oh, the one at the zoo looked scary, all right, but my brother, Cameron and I would soon have an experience with California condors in the wild.

An experience that still gives me shivers to this day.

The school year ended, and, two weeks later, we started planning for our family vacation. Every summer we travel to northern California to Mt. Shasta to go camping in the foothills. Mt. Shasta is a long, long drive from Los Angeles.

But it's so much fun! The four of us—Mom, Dad, Cameron and I—camp in tents for a week. We go back to the same place every year. There are no houses, cars, or people. Just the four of us and the forest. We hike, fish, swim, and roast marshmallows at night. It's a blast!

But my favorite part is this:

In the foothills of Mt. Shasta, where we camp, I pan for gold in some of the mountain streams, and I've actually found real gold! Usually it's just tiny specks or flakes that aren't worth much money, but I don't care. I have a ton of fun panning for gold.

And this year was going to be even better, because I bought a metal detector with the money I'd made at my lemonade stand last summer. I was hoping that the metal detector would help me locate even bigger pieces of gold near some of the streams.

Wouldn't that be cool? To find a big gold nugget?

Cameron isn't really into gold panning. This year, he got a remote control airplane for his birthday, and he brought it with us on the trip so he could fly it around. But he had a problem the very moment he tried to get it off the ground.

"What's wrong with this thing?" he said to himself, turning the switch on and off. We had just finished unpacking the car and pitching the tents. Cameron and I had our own tent, and Mom and Dad had a tent right next to ours. I was testing out my metal detector, sweeping it over a can. The detector is sort of like a big golf club with a flat, round disc at the bottom. When you sweep the disc over metal, the machine makes a beeping sound.

I swept it over an unopened can of baked beans.

Beep—beep—beep.

"Cool!" I exclaimed.

"Yeah, well, *this* isn't so cool," Cameron said angrily.

"What's wrong?" I asked.

"This goofy plane won't work. The remote control works fine, but the plane won't turn on."

"Did you put in new batteries?" I asked.

A funny look came over Cameron's face. Then, with his free hand, he slapped his palm to his forehead.

"Batteries!" he cried. "I forgot to bring fresh batteries!"

"Bummer," I said.

"I can't believe I forgot them!" he exclaimed. "I had them right on my dresser."

"Double bummer," I said.

Cameron stuffed the remote control unit in his back pocket, carried the plane to the car, and he put it in the backseat.

"I guess that won't be much good for the rest of the week," he said with dismay.

"Want to go hunt for gold with me?" I asked.

"You never find much," he said, sitting on a stump. "It sounds boring."

"Hey, you never know," I said. "Now that I've got this metal detector, I might find a huge hunk of gold. I could get rich!"

Cameron shrugged. He's two years younger than me—I'm twelve, he's ten—and I kind of felt sorry for him. He was really planning on flying his airplane.

"Come on," I urged. "It'll be fun. You can pan for gold in the stream, and I'll use my metal detector on the riverbank. You never know . . . we just might find some gold."

Cameron stood up. "I guess it beats hanging around here," he said.

Mom and Dad were on the other side of their tent, preparing a place to make a fire.

"Mom," I said, "Can Cameron and I go look for gold?"

Mom stepped out from behind the tent. "Yeah," she replied, squinting in the bight sun. "Remember, just like last year: follow the stream so you don't get lost. Cameron, do you have your watch?"

Cameron held his arm up, displaying his wristwatch.

"Okay," Mom continued, looking at her own watch. "It's noon . . . be back here by four o'clock to get ready for dinner. And remember to take your canteens of water."

Four o'clock?!?! I thought. *That's four hours! We've got all afternoon to hunt for gold!*

186

I dug into my pack and found a small bottle that I use to carry gold in. Since I usually find tiny flecks of gold, I didn't really need to have anything bigger. And if we *were* lucky enough to find a bigger nugget, I could always carry it.

I stuffed the small bottle in my front pocket of my jeans, picked up my canteen, and clipped it to my belt loop. Then I picked up my pan that I use to look for gold. Cameron found his canteen and took a sip before he, too, clipped it to his belt loop. I handed him the pan.

"Ready?" I asked.

"Let's go," he said. "By Mom! By Dad! See you in a while!"

Mom and Dad waved, and Cameron and I turned and walked to the small stream that runs next to our camp site. It's only about as wide as a car and only a few feet deep.

And I didn't waste any time, either. I turned on my metal detector and immediately began sweeping it back and forth at the edge of the stream. Cameron knelt down on the riverbank and scooped up a pile of sand from the bottom of the stream, swishing it around until only the heaviest objects remained. That's how you pan for gold: if there's any gold in the pile of dirt in your pan, it will stay on the bottom. All of the lighter materials—sand and small pebbles—get washed away.

But we didn't have much luck. Slowly, we made our way farther and farther downstream. I continued with the metal detector, but I still hadn't found anything. Cameron was getting bored. He'd stopped panning altogether, and was just looking down into the stream as we walked.

"You're not going to find any gold that way," I said.

And it was at that exact moment that his arm suddenly shot out. His eyes widened, and his jaw dropped.

"Oh my gosh!" he exclaimed. *"Look at that!"*

And when I saw what he was pointing at, I couldn't believe my eyes.

3

Me and my big mouth. I had just told my brother that he'd never find any gold without panning for it—but now we stood on the riverbank, looking at a shiny nugget of gold, gleaming back at us like a brilliant yellow eye from the bottom of the stream.

Cameron was so excited that he fell to his knees and thrust his arm into the water, soaking his shirt sleeve. He pulled his hand out of the water, stood up and opened his fist.

"Wow!" I shrieked. "I can't believe it!"

In his hand was a gold nugget, nearly the size of a pea. Now, you may not think that's very big, but let me tell you . . . a pea-sized gold nugget is considered huge.

"How much do you think it's worth?" Cameron asked excitedly.

"A lot!" I said. "Probably around twenty bucks!"

"Twenty bucks?!?!" he exclaimed. "And you said I wouldn't find any gold without using the pan!"

He shoved the gold nugget into his pocket, and we returned our gazes to the stream. If we found one nugget, there might be more.

"I can't believe you found that," I said. "I've never found a nugget that big."

"I'm going to find another one," Cameron said.

"As much as I'd like to find one, I think the chances aren't very good. That nugget was probably visible because the river has washed it downstream. Maybe we should head upstream and see if we could find where it came from."

"Not me," Cameron said, shaking his head. "If there's one nugget here, I'll bet there's more."

We searched and searched. While we walked, I kept the metal detector on, sweeping the disc-shaped foot a few inches above the ground. It never made a sound.

And we didn't see any more nuggets in the stream, either. Cameron went back to panning, but he found nothing.

Until—

"Wait a minute," he said, peering into the muddy pan. "I think I saw something."

I knelt down next to him. Cameron gently swished his fingers through the sand, sifting it away with the water.

"What did you see?" I asked.

"A shark," he remarked smartly.

"Yeah, right," I said, rolling my eyes.

"I saw something shiny. I did, really."

He sifted some more. Sure enough, we suddenly saw a shiny glint of light from the bottom of the pan—but when Cameron plucked it out with his thumb and forefinger, we discovered it was only a shiny piece of quartz. Quartz is a type of stone, and it can be really shiny, like glass.

"Bummer," I said with a sigh. Then I looked up and saw something that was so unexpected—so shocking—that the only thing I could do was stare.

I gasped.

"C . . . Cameron," I stammered quietly. "Move very slowly . . . and look up in that tree over there."

Cameron did as asked, and when he saw what I was looking at, his whole body shook.

"That's . . . that's—"

"That's a California condor!" I said, finishing his sentence.

Neither one of us could say anything more. Thirty feet away, sitting on a low branch, was a gigantic California condor . . . just like the one we'd seen at the Los Angeles Zoo

Except for one thing.

The condor at the zoo had looked a little scary. Maybe because it was so big and strange looking.

The bird we were looking at in the tree, however, looked *angry*.

It looked *mean*.

That's crazy, I thought. *How can a condor be mean? It's just a bird.*

But Cameron sensed the same thing.

"Melanie," he whispered, *"take a look at its eyes. He looks like he's really mad at us or something."*

Cameron was right! The condor was looking at us like we had done something wrong . . . and maybe we had.

"Cameron," I said, "we have to get out of here. We might be near the bird's nest. If we are, the condor might feel threatened, even though we aren't going to try to hurt it."

All of a sudden, the enormous bird slowly spread its wings. It moved cautiously, watching us with those piercing, cold eyes. I felt a terrible chill.

Then the condor just sort of dipped forward. Its huge wings caught air, and the bird was suddenly swooping through the sky . . . away from us.

I let out a sigh of relief. Cameron did, too.

"That was so cool!" he said. "Wait until we tell Mom and Dad!"

"I wish we could have taken a picture," I said. "Not many people can say they've seen a real, live California condor in the wild."

Now we had *two* things to be excited about.

First, Cameron had found a gold nugget, which was really cool. Every once in a while he would take it out of his pocket and look at it.

And second, we saw a real, live, honest-to-goodness California condor.

"That thing really scared me for a minute," Cameron said.

"Me, too," I agreed. "He sure looked frightening. But we'll probably never see a California condor in the wild again."

Well, I was wrong about Cameron finding gold. I had told him that he wouldn't find any gold without panning, and I was wrong.

And I was wrong about the condor.

We would see it again . . . sooner than I'd ever imagined.

5

Cameron looked at his watch.

"Gosh, it's only twelve-thirty," he said. "We still have a lot of time left to hunt for gold."

And that's what we did. We continued along the stream, scouring the riverbank with the metal detector and panning in the stream. Cameron and I took turns, but we didn't have any luck. Panning for gold would be a hard way to make a living.

"Let's take a break," Cameron said, wiping the sweat from his forehead. He un-clipped his canteen of water from his belt loop and took a sip. I did the same, and we found a spot in the shade and sat down.

Cameron dug into his pocket and pulled out the gold nugget. He held it in his hand, inspecting it.

"Hard to believe they make coins out of this stuff," he said.

"And jewelry," I added. "Think about it, Cam. Over a hundred years ago, there might have been miners panning for gold in this very spot. When gold was discovered in California, people came from all over the world to find their fortune. Some people found gold nuggets the size of bowling balls."

Cameron let out a whistle. "That would be awesome," he said. "We'd be rich! I could buy a brand new car!"

"You can't even *drive*," I reminded him.

"Yeah, but it sure would be cool to be the only kid in school that had his own car. I could have Mom drive me to school and pick me up every day."

"Oh, I'm sure she'd *love* to do that," I said with a smirk.

"What would you do if you found a gold nugget that big?" he asked.

Good question.

"I guess I would save the money for college or something," I replied.

"Get out of here!" he said, recoiling. "You mean to tell me that you wouldn't spend *any* of it?!?!"

"Well, I might. I might buy some clothes and some compact discs."

"I'd buy a sports car," Cameron said, making noises like a car engine. "One that goes super-fast. *That's* what *I* would buy."

That's my brother for you.

"Well, we aren't going to find any gold sitting here in the shade," I said. "Come on."

We stood. I picked up my metal detector and began sweeping it just above the ground. Cameron walked to the edge of the stream and began dipping the pan into the water.

"Hey! I caught a fish in the pan!" he exclaimed.

I walked to where he was kneeling and bent over.

Sure enough, a small fish was darting around in the pan.

"Maybe we could take it back to Mom and Dad and tell them that we caught dinner," I said with a smirk. Cameron laughed, tilting the pan sideways to let the fish escape.

But then he stopped laughing. He was staring down into the water with a horrified look upon his face.

"What is it?" I asked, thinking that maybe he saw a snake. Cameron is terrified of snakes.

I looked down into the stream, but I didn't see anything that would cause Cameron to freak out.

Then, as I continued looking, I realized that it wasn't something in the *water* that Cameron was looking at.

It was a *reflection* in the water.

Something big.

And dark.

Something from above was coming at us, and fast.

A shadow suddenly fell over us, and I turned and looked up.

A California condor.

He was coming right at us, claws bared, beak wide.

And those *eyes*.

Cold, lifeless eyes glared at us.

Angry eyes that burned with fury.

When we studied California condors in school, we learned that they don't attack people. Period.

But this condor *was* attacking, and I knew already there was no way we could escape the terrible beast as it hurled toward us at lightning speed. The only thing I could do was close my eyes . . . and scream.

FUN FACTS ABOUT VERMONT:

State Capitol: Montpelier

State Butterfly: Monarch

State Nickname: Green Mountain State

State Animal: Morgan Horse

State Bird: Hermit Thrush

State Motto: "Freedom and Unity"

State Tree: Sugar Maple

State Insect: Honeybee

State Flower: Red Clover

Statehood: March 4th, 1791 (14th state)

FAMOUS PEOPLE FROM VERMONT!

Chester Arthur, 21st US President

Calvin Coolidge, 30th US President

**Ben Cohen/Jerry Greenfield, makers of
Ben & Jerry's Ice Cream**

**Brigham Young, Colonizer and
Territorial Governor**

Orson Bean, actor

Katherine Paterson, children's author

John Dewey, Philosopher

Rudy Vallee, singer and band leader

Elisha Graves Otis, inventor of the elevator

among many, many more!

Also by Johnathan Rand:

GHOST IN THE GRAVEYARD

ABOUT THE AUTHOR

Johnathan Rand is the author of more than 50 books, with well over 2 million copies in print. Series include **AMERICAN CHILLERS, MICHIGAN CHILLERS, FREDDIE FERNORTNER, FEARLESS FIRST GRADER**, and **THE ADVENTURE CLUB.** He's also co-authored a novel for teens (with Christopher Knight) entitled **PANDEMIA**. When not traveling, Rand lives in northern Michigan with his wife and two dogs. He is also the only author in the world to have a store that sells only his works: **CHILLERMANIA!** is located in Indian River, Michigan. Johnathan Rand is not always at the store, but he has been known to drop by frequently. Find out more at:

www.americanchillers.com

ATTENTION YOUNG AUTHORS!
DON'T MISS

JOHNATHAN RAND'S

AUTHOR QUEST

THE DEFINITIVE WRITER'S CAMP
FOR SERIOUS YOUNG WRITERS

If you want to sharpen your writing skills, become a better writer, and have a blast, Johnathan Rand's Author Quest is for you!

Designed exclusively for young writers, Author Quest is 4 days/3 nights of writing courses, instruction, and classes at Camp Ocqueoc, nestled in the secluded wilds of northern lower Michigan. Oh, there are lots of other fun indoor and outdoor activities, too . . . but the main focus of Author Quest is about becoming an even better writer! Instructors include published authors and (of course!) Johnathan Rand. No matter what kind of writing you enjoy: fiction, non-fiction, fantasy, thriller/horror, humor, mystery, history . . . this camp is designed for writers who have this in common: they LOVE to write, and they want to improve their skills!

For complete details and an application, visit:

www.americanchillers.com

Join the official

AMERICAN

CHILLERS

FAN CLUB!

Visit www.americanchillers.com for details!

Johnathan Rand travels internationally for school visits and book signings! For booking information, call:

1 (231) 238-0338!

www.americanchillers.com

All AudioCraft books are proudly printed, bound, and manufactured in the United States of America, utilizing American resources, labor, and materials.

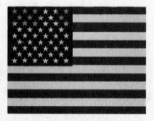

USA